W0371795

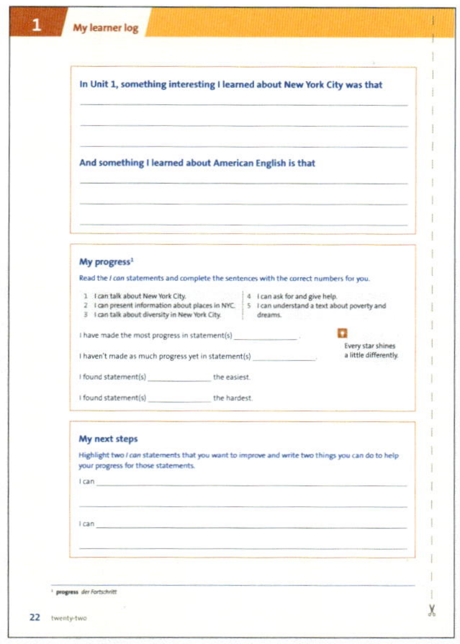

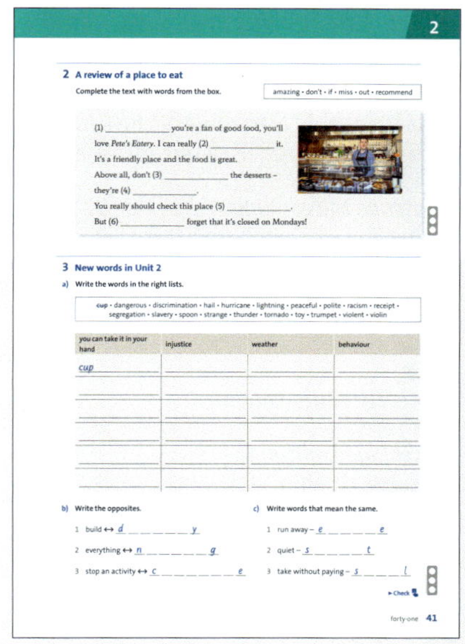

Wordpower

Auf diesen Seiten findest du Übungen zu den Vokabeln der jeweiligen Units und kannst dein gesprochenes Englisch verbessern.

My learner log

Hier kannst du auf die Unit zurückblicken und deinen Lernstand festhalten.

Revision

Halte auf diesen Seiten inne und wiederhole, was du in den vorherigen Units gelernt hast.

Dein Buch findest du auch in der Cornelsen Lernen App

Siehst du eines dieser Symbole in deinem Workbook, kannst du in deiner App …

Erklär-film

Hörtexte, Videos und Erklärfilme zu deinem Workbook anhören und anschauen.

► Digital help

dir Hilfe holen, z. B.:
- Satzanfänge und Ideen
- Checklisten
- Aufgabenerklärungen zum Anhören

► Check

deine Antworten eigenständig überprüfen.

lighthouse 4
BASIC

Workbook

Im Auftrag des Verlages erarbeitet von
Sydney Thorne, York; Zoe Thorne, Royston

In Zusammenarbeit mit der Englischredaktion
Klaus Unger (Projektleitung),
Karin Wedepohl (verantwortliche Redakteurin), Jenny Dames,
Michael Dunkel, Chelsea Ledvinka-Heß, Julian Theo Wacker

Beratende Mitwirkung
Sabine Bay, Cloppenburg; Ulrike Plänker, Sprockhövel

Illustrationen
Yaroslaw Schwarzstein, Hannover

Fotos
Chocolate Films, London

Umschlaggestaltung
Rosendahl, Berlin

Layoutkonzept
Klein & Halm, Berlin

Layout und technische Umsetzung
PER MEDIEN & MARKETING GmbH, Braunschweig

www.cornelsen.de

Druck: Athesiadruck GmbH, Bozen

1. Auflage, 1. Druck 2025
Workbook 4
ISBN 978-3-06-036701-6

1. Auflage, 1. Druck 2025
Workbook 4 Lehrkräftefassung
ISBN 978-3-06-036697-2

PEFC-zertifiziert
Dieses Produkt stammt aus nachhaltig bewirtschafteten Wäldern und kontrollierten Quellen
PEFC/18-31-166
www.pefc.de

BASIC

lighthouse 4

Workbook

Audios online verfügbar unter
www.cornelsen.de/webcodes **Code:** davaco

Dein Workbook findest du auch in der **Cornelsen Lernen App**.
Siehst du eines dieser Symbole in deinem Workbook, findest du in der App …

alle **Audios**

alle **Videos** und **Erklärfilme**

Hilfen und **Lösungen** zu ausgewählten Aufgaben

Cornelsen

Titelbild

Statue: stock.adobe.com/Oleksandr Dibrova; Personen: Chocolate Films: Hintergrund: stock.adobe.com/wajan

Illustrationen

Cornelsen/Inhouse/Melina Frick: **S. 18, 27, 81**; Cornelsen/Jaroslav Schwarzstein: **S. 12**, **S. 20**, **S. 28**, **S. 52**, **S. 56**, **S. 59**/u., **S. 60**, **S. 72**, **S. 76**/r., **S. 77**/l.

Fotos

S. 3: Cornelsen/Inhouse/Anne Weingarten; **S. 5**/o.: stock.adobe.com/f11photo; **S. 5**/2.v.o.: stock.adobe.com/SeanPavonePhoto; **S. 5**/3.v.o.: Shutterstock.com/Daniel M Ernst; **S. 5**/4.v.o.: stock.adobe.com/Aerial Film Studio; **S. 5**/u.: stock.adobe.com/surangaw; **S. 6**/o.: stock.adobe.com/martialred; **S. 6**/u.: stock.adobe.com/sebi_2569; **S. 7**: Depositphotos/SYEDA RUMANA FERDOUS. BRISTY; **S. 8**: imago sport/Newscom World; **S. 9**: Shutterstock.com/New Africa; **S. 10**: Imago Stock & People GmbH/Shotshop; **S. 11**: Imago Stock & People GmbH/dreamstime; **S. 13**/A: stock.adobe.com/exclusive-design; **S. 13**/B: stock.adobe.com/Markus Mainka; **S. 13**/C: stock.adobe.com/ange1011; erzeugt mit generativer KI; **S. 13**/D: stock.adobe.com/thodonal; **S. 13**/E: Shutterstock.com/AS Food studio; **S. 13**/F: Shutterstock.com/Philip Kinsey; **S. 15**: mauritius images/Cinema-Legacy-Collection; **S. 16**: Shutterstock.com/enterlinedesign; **S. 17**/o.: stock.adobe.com/Bobboz; **S. 17**/u.: Shutterstock.com/Kochnieva Karyna; **S. 24**: mauritius images/Kevin Bennett/Alamy/Alamy Stock Photos; **S. 25**/m.: Shutterstock.com/AYO Production; **S. 25**/u.: Shutterstock.com/Muangsatun; **S. 26**: Shutterstock.com/Grommik; **S. 30**: mauritius images/IanDagnall Computing/Alamy Stock Photos; **S. 31**: interfoto e.k.; **S. 32**: Shutterstock.com/Jacek Chabraszewski; **S. 33**/A: mauritius images/Anton Starikov/Alamy; **S. 33**/B: Shutterstock.com/MaraZe; **S. 33**/C: stock.adobe.com/Africa Studio; **S. 33**/D: stock.adobe.com/supamas; **S. 33**/E: stock.adobe.com/Wander Taste; **S. 33**/F: Shutterstock.com/grey_and; **S. 35**: Cornelsen/Inhouse, Jenny Dames/Digital Learning Ass. Ltd.; **S. 40**: stock.adobe.comDOMHOUZE; **S. 41**: Shutterstock.com/Dan Rentea; **S. 42**: mauritius images/Alpha Stock/Alamy; **S. 43**: mauritius images/Minden Pictures; **S. 44**: Cornelsen/Mädchen mit Gedankenwolke: Shutterstock.com/MillaF, Hausreihe r.: Shutterstock.com/bodhichita, Haus m.: stock.adobe.com/stock.adobe.comStudioATC, Terrasse l.: Imago Stock & People GmbH/depositphoto; **S. 46**/1: Shutterstock.com/Roman Samborskyi; **S. 46**/2: Shutterstock.com/Pixel-Shot; **S. 46**/3: stock.adobe.com/Simone; **S. 46**/4: Imago Stock & People GmbH/imago images/Image Source; **S. 46**/5: Shutterstock.com/BearFotos; **S. 46**/6: Shutterstock.com/Ground Picture; **S. 46**/Ikon: stock.adobe.com/Cali6ro; **S. 47**/Ikons erstaunt + Herz: Shutterstock.com/Carboxylase; **S. 47**/Ikons Hände + Muffin + traurig: stock.adobe.com/Cali6ro; **S. 47**/o.r.: Shutterstock.com/James Kirkikis; **S. 48**/o.: Shutterstock.com/KTracePhotography; **S. 48**/u.: Shutterstock.com/KTracePhotography; **S. 51**/Ikon A: Shutterstock.com/Carboxylase; **S. 51**/Ikons B-F: stock.adobe.com/Cali6ro; **S. 58**: stock.adobe.com/Tupungato; **S. 59**/o.: mauritius images/Matt Gush/Alamy Stock Photos; **S. 61**: Shutterstock.com/SeventyFour; **S. 62**: Imago Stock & People GmbH/Imagebroker; **S. 63**/2.v.o.: akg-images/UIG/Marka; **S. 63**/3.v.o.: akg-images/De Agostini Picture Library; **S. 63**/4.v.o.: Shutterstock.com/val lawless; **S. 63**/o.: stock.adobe.com/top/s/s-top; **S. 63**/u.: akg-images; **S. 64**: Tyler Glasses Jr.; **S. 65**: CartoonStock/Rich Diesslin; **S. 66**: Shutterstock.com/zaranda; **S. 67**: Cornelsen/Inhouse, Jenny Dames/SWIMMING IN THE DESERT by Alvaro Ron, USA, 2017, 18 min/interfilm Berlin Management GmbH; **S. 68**/1: Shutterstock.com/Freaktography; **S. 68**/2+6: mauritius images/Minden Pictures; **S. 68**/3: Shutterstock.com/Photo_Time; **S. 68**/4: mauritius images/Robert Harding; **S. 68**/5: Shutterstock.com/noorun; **S. 69**: mauritius images/Tomasz Zajda/Alamy Stock Photos; **S. 71**: Cornelsen/Inhouse/KI-generiert mit Bing Image Creator (Dall-e 3); **S. 72**: stock.adobe.com/Nicholas Felix/peopleimages.com; **S. 74**/o.: Shutterstock.com/Pixel-Shot; **S. 74**/u.: Shutterstock.com/VictorH11; **S. 75**/o.: Shutterstock.com/Sublimage; **S. 75**/u.: Shutterstock.com/Tony LePrieur Photography; **S. 76**/r.: mauritius images/BLM Collection/Alamy; **S. 77**/l.: akg-images/Science Source; **S. 78**/1, l.: Shutterstock.com/JULIANA WILLIAMS. **S. 78**/1, m.: Shutterstock.com/kochabamba; **S. 78**/10: Shutterstock.com/biletskiyevgeniy.com; **S. 78**/2: Shutterstock.com/IrinaShamanaeva; **S. 78**/3: Shutterstock.com/Tom Tietz; **S. 78**/4: Shutterstock.com/You Touch Pix of EuToch; **S. 78**/5: Shutterstock.com/Tony LePrieur Photography; **S. 78**/6: Shutterstock.com/Tory Kallman; **S. 78**/7: Shutterstock.com/Artem Onoprienko; **S. 78**/8: Shutterstock.com/Boris Stroujko; **S. 78**/9: Shutterstock.com/CatwalkPhotos; **S. 80**/A+B+D: Imago Stock & People GmbH/imago images/Cover-Images; **S. 80**/C: Imago Stock & People GmbH/Cover-Images; **S. 81**/m.l.: stock.adobe.com/Sergii Figurnyi; **S. 82**/2.v.l.: Shutterstock.com/MaraZe; **S. 82**/3.v.l.: stock.adobe.com/Africa Studio; **S. 82**/4.v.l.: stock.adobe.com/supamas; **S. 82**/l.: mauritius images/Anton Starikov/Alamy; **S. 82**/r.: stock.adobe.com/Wander Taste

Datenquellen

S. 8: Der Text basiert auf Daten aus: The Nation's Report Card: NAEP Report Card: U.S. History, https://www.nationsreportcard.gov/ushistory/results/achievement/ (Zugriff: 28.04.2025); **S. 13**: Das Diagramm basiert auf Daten aus dem Bericht des NYC City Comptroller, Countries of Origin of New York City Immigrants, https://comptroller.nyc.gov/reports/our-immigrantpopulation-helps-power-nyc-economy/ (Zugriff: 30.04.2025); **S. 78**: Das Diagramm basiert auf Daten der Mesriani Law Group, https://www.mesrianilaw.com/blog/californiacaraccident-statistics/ (Zugriff: 30.04.2025)

Welcome to the USA

1 READING Find the state

▸ SB, pp. 10–11

a) **Read the sentences and use the map on pages 10–11 of your book to find the correct state.**

1 This state is in the south of the USA, west of Lousiana. ____________

2 This state is on the west coast of the USA and it is south of Oregon. ____________

3 This state is in the centre of the USA, between Colorado and Missouri. ____________

4 This state is in the north-east of the USA, north of Pennsylvania. ____________

5 This state is on the east coast of the USA and it is east of Tennessee. ____________

b) **Write two more sentences about states, using the phrases in blue in a) to help you.**

1 *This state is* ____________

2 ____________

c) **Ask a partner to find the two states.**

2 READING All about one state

▸ SB, p. 11

Read the text and complete the information.

State: ____________

Where it is: ____________

____

Also called: ____________

Biggest cities: ____________

State drink: ____________

State flag description: ____________

____

Arizona

Arizona is a large state in the south-west of the USA, between California and Texas. It is sometimes called 'the Grand Canyon State' because of its most famous sight. The biggest cities are Phoenix and Tucson. Summers are very hot in Arizona, so the state drink is – lemonade!

3 An American puzzle

▸ SB, p. 13

a) **Complete the puzzle with the American words and places.**

1 An activity that you can do in the sea.

2 A US state where you can find alligators.

3 The colour of the stars on the American flag.

4 *(across)* A place with lots of film studios.

5 *(down)* Islands make this American state.

6 The leader of the USA.

7 The money used in the USA.

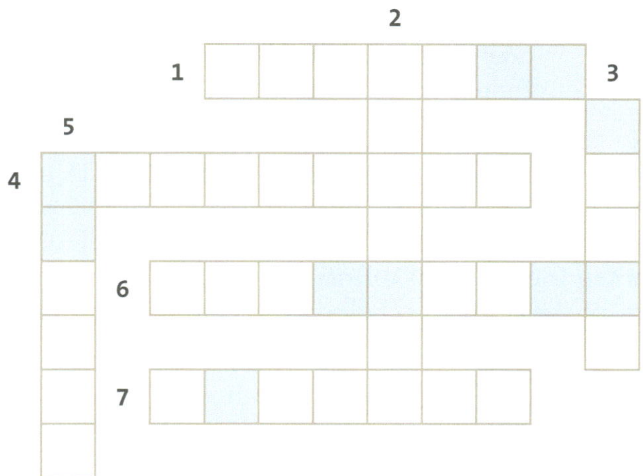

b) **Put the letters in the blue boxes into the right order to find the family name of the first American president.**

___ ___ ___ ___ ___ ___ ___ ___ ___ ___

4 Reading Germany and the USA

▸ SB, pp. 12–13

Complete the text with the correct information from the quiz in your book on pages 12–13.

Germany and the USA have some things that are similar, for example both countries have states: Germany has 16 states and the USA has (1) ________________ states. Both countries also have a leader called the (2) ________________, but they have different roles. Other things are different too, for example the USA is (3) ________________ times bigger than Germany. The USA also has a lot (4) ________________ people – about 84 million people live in Germany, but over (5) ________________ people live in the USA!

5 Reading An American musical

▸ SB, p. 13

a) Read the article and say if each sentence is true (T), false (F) or not in the text (N).

Hip-Hop History

Do you know why most people in the USA speak English? Or do you know why American money is called a dollar? If the answer is no, you are not alone! Only 13% of teens in the USA know a lot about their country's history. But this is changing, thanks to – a musical!

Hamilton is one of the most successful musicals of all time and has won 11 prizes. The musical tells the story of Alexander Hamilton who was a poor man on a small island in the Caribbean[1]. And he was poor when he came to the USA in 1772, when the USA was a British colony[2]. But, amazingly, he became one of the seven 'Fathers' of the USA who helped the country become free from Great Britain in 1776.

Hamilton is a very different musical in many ways. First, it is a hip-hop musical, so most of the words are in rap. Also, most of the actors in this musical are Black or have immigrant backgrounds because this helps people to remember that immigrants[3] have always been important to the USA, both today and in the past.

Lots of schools have programs where students can watch the musical and have classes with the actors where they learn more about this time in history. One student said, 'I usually find history really boring, but it's so interesting to learn about it this way. Now I just need a hip-hop musical to explain math and science and I'll get an A in school!'

Datenquelle: https://www.nationsreportcard.gov/ushistory/results/achievement/ (siehe Quellenverzeichnis)

1 Most teens in the USA know lots about American history. ☐

2 *Hamilton* is a very popular musical. ☐

3 Alexander Hamilton was born in the USA. ☐

4 The USA was part of Great Britain in the past. ☐

5 There are a lot of actors in the musical. ☐

6 Many students find the musical helpful for their history lessons. ☐

☒ b) Have you seen or would you like to see *Hamilton*? Why or why not?

I saw ______________________________

Yes, I'd ______________________________

No, I wouldn't ______________________________

[1] **Caribbean** *die Karibik* [2] **colony** *die Kolonie* [3] **immigrant** *der/die Immigrant/in*

6 At summer camp

► SB, pp. 14–15

Look at pages 14–15 in your book. Then look at the sentences below. Who could say each sentence: Amy, Troy, Diego or Tiana? Write the names.

______ *I'm from a state in the south. I'd like to try a different hobby or sport.*

My family are Native American and I love making things. ______

______ *I'm from a big city, so I want to try something new outdoors, and also eat something delicious!*

I like all sorts of things to do with computers and I'm looking forward to doing a hobby outside. ______

7 The camp timetable

► Digital help ► SB, p. 15

a) Read the sentences. Complete the timetable for the summer camp with the activities in the box.

1 The first activity of the week is climbing.
2 On Wednesday morning, you can look for animals.
3 Thursday afternoon is good for people who like art.
4 The last activity of the week is singing together.
5 The activities that start with 'k' are both on the same day.
6 Both the activities on Wednesday are connected to animals.
7 The swimming lessons are before the painting class.
8 There is a water sport on Monday afternoon.
9 The hike comes before learning how to make great photos.

bird watching • ~~climbing~~ • catch fish • hiking • karaoke • kayaking • painting • photography • swimming lessons • windsurfing

	in the morning	in the afternoon
Monday	*go climbing*	*go*
Tuesday	*go*	*make*
Wednesday	*do*	*catch*
Thursday	*have*	*do*
Friday	*go*	*have*

b) What activities would you do at your dream summer camp? What wouldn't you do? Why?

At my dream summer camp, I would ______

I wouldn't ______ *because* ______

I can talk about the USA.

Unit 1
NYC: The world in a city

1 New York City (NYC) with Annalise

► SB, p. 16–17

Watch the video. Are the sentences true (T) or false (F)?

1 Annalise often goes to the farmers' market in Union Square. ☐
2 It's hard to get to Union Square because not many subway[1] lines go there. ☐
3 Annalise's favourite ice cream is Sicilian[2] lemon. ☐
4 In the West Village Annalise meets her friends in a coffee shop or pizzeria. ☐
5 Annalise thinks watching basketball games is a bit boring. ☐
6 The *Strand Bookstore* opened in 1927. ☐
7 A problem in New York is that almost everybody has a car. ☐
8 Koreatown is one long street. ☐

2 A New York City poem

► SB, p. 17

Read Annalise's poem about New York and choose the right words from the box to complete it. There are more words than you need.

eat • food • night • proud • small • street • tall • white

New York is the place to meet
With yellow taxis in the (1) ______________.
Times Square is great, both day and (2) ______________,
A mix of noises, colours, lights.
From Union Square to Koreatown,
We have the best (3) ______________ of any town!
The Statue of Liberty stands proud and (4) ______________,
A symbol[3] that we welcome all.
And that is why I'm (5) ______________ to be
A New Yorker – I ♥ NYC!

[1] **subway** *die U-Bahn* [2] **Sicilian** *sizilianisch* [3] **symbol** *das Symbol*

I can talk about New York City.

3 New York City sights

▸ SB, p. 18

Read the sentences and write the correct sight in New York City (NYC).

Central Park • One WTC • Statue of Liberty • Times Square • Washington Square Park

1 This woman with a light in her hand is the symbol of NYC. *the* ______________________

2 This is an area with lots of big screens. It's always very busy. ______________________

3 A place where New Yorkers remember people who died. ______________________

4 A place where you can often see street musicians. ______________________

5 This is the largest green area in the middle of the city. ______________________

4 MEDIATION The Staten Island Ferry

▸ SB, p. 19

You are visiting NYC with your family, and they have found information about the Staten Island Ferry. Read the information and complete the fact file in German.

Fact file: Die *Staten Island* Fähre

Uhrzeiten:

____

____

Empfohlene Reisezeit für Touristen:

____

____

Sehenswürdigkeiten auf *Staten Island*:

____

____

Fahrradmitnahme erlaubt? ______________________

Warnung: Es wird vor Menschen gewarnt, die

____

______________________.

THE STATEN ISLAND FERRY

Take the ferry – the best way to travel between Manhattan and Staten Island!

The ferry runs 24 hours a day, 7 days a week. Normally there are ferries every 30 minutes, but during rush hour (6 a.m. to 9:30 a.m. and from 3:30 p.m. to 8:00 p.m. on weekdays) they are every 15 minutes. But remember the ferries will be busy during this time as lots of people use them to get to and from work! If you want to visit the many sights on Staten Island, like the zoo, parks or museums, it's best to travel at a different time.
Bikes, but not cars, are allowed on the ferries.

WARNING Be careful! Some people try to sell tickets to tourists for a few dollars – but the ferry is free!

5 A tour of Manhattan

► SB, p. 19

a) **Look at the map and complete the text with words from the box.**

across • along • Ferry • left • Liberty • north • on • right • Station

Start at the Brooklyn Bridge. Then turn (1) __________ and go straight (2) __________ all the way to Battery Park. This is where you can take the Staten Island (3) __________. From the (4) __________ end of Battery Park, go north and you'll come to One WTC. Look (5) __________ the river here to see the Statue of (6) __________. Go north, then turn (7) __________ and then left and you'll come to Washington Square Park. Go north (8) __________ 5th Avenue until you get to the Empire State Building. Go north again, then turn right into 42nd Street and you'll come to the Grand Central (9) __________.

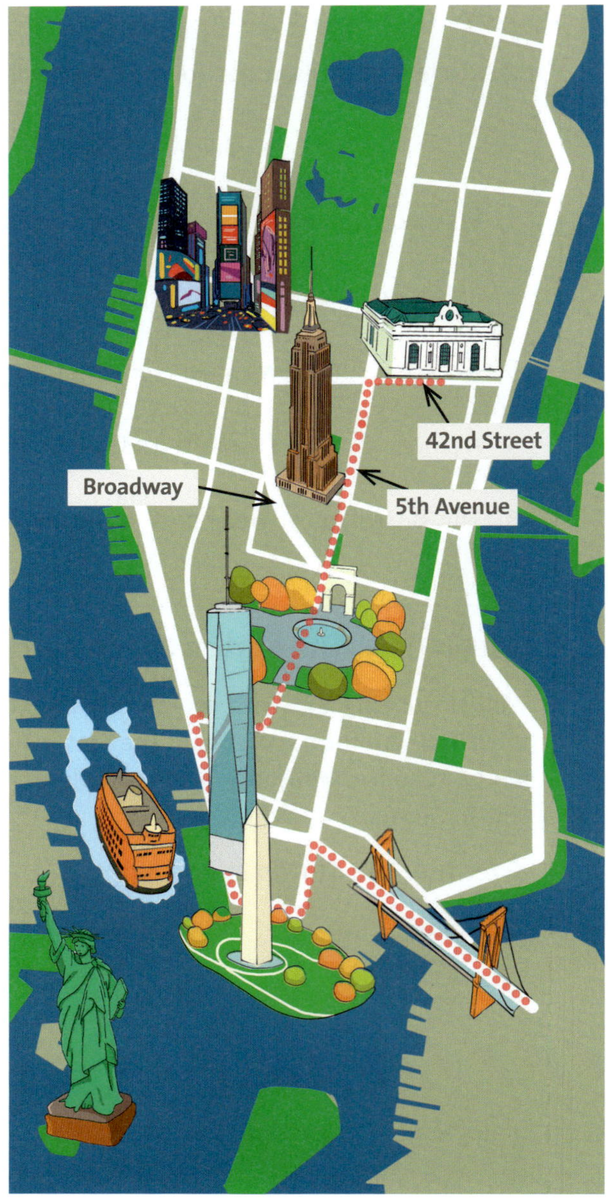

b) **Write directions[1] from where you are now to ...**

1 Central Park:

____

2 Times Square:

____

[1] **directions** *die Wegbeschreibung(en)*

I can talk about places in NYC.

6 LISTENING Where New Yorkers come from

01 ▸ SB, p. 20

Population of NYC: 8.2 million

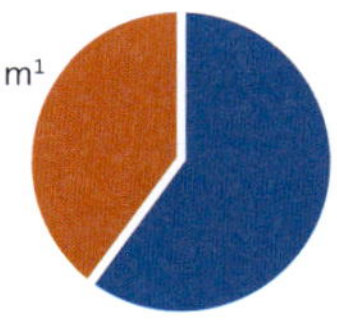

a) BEFORE YOU LISTEN **Look at the diagram.**

1 What is the total number of people in NYC? ____________

2 What is the number of New Yorkers who were born outside the USA? ____________

3 How many New Yorkers were born in the USA? ____________

b) **Listen to the radio report[2] and complete the text with the correct numbers and countries.**

The 3.3 million New Yorkers who were born outside the USA come from more than 150 different countries. For example:

1 Caribbean and Central America

13.7 % were born in the Dominican Republic.

_____ % were born in Jamaica.

5.4% were born in ____________.

2 Asia

_____ % were born in China.

2.7% were born in ____________.

3 Europe

1.6% were born in Poland.

2.7% were born in Italy, ____________

and the ____________.

4 Other countries

And _____ % of New Yorkers born outside of the USA were born in other countries.

7 WORDS Food words in NYC

▸ SB, p. 20

1 Arabic • 2 German • 3 Italian • ~~4 Spanish~~ • 5 Turkish • 6 Yiddish

a) **Match the food words (A-F) to the languages they come from (1-6).**

A  pizza ☐

B  kebab ☐

C  bagel ☐

D  pretzel ☐

E  falafel ☐

F  paella 4

b) **Compare with a partner. Can you agree on your answers?**

c) SPEAKING **Tell your partner which of these foods you have tried, and what you thought of them.**

I've tried ... and I really liked ...

I have never tried ... Have you? What's it like?

d) **Add any more food words from other languages that you can think of.**

____

[1] **m (= million)** *die Million(en)* [2] **radio report** *der Radiobericht*

8 LANGUAGE Twenty verbs in the simple past

► SB, p. 22

a) Write the verbs in the simple past.

1 break 2 keep 3 know 4 make 5 put 6 teach 7 hear 8 wear 9 write 10 catch 11 tell 12 see 13 begin 14 become 15 buy 16 eat 17 sell 18 go 19 give 20 bring 21 think

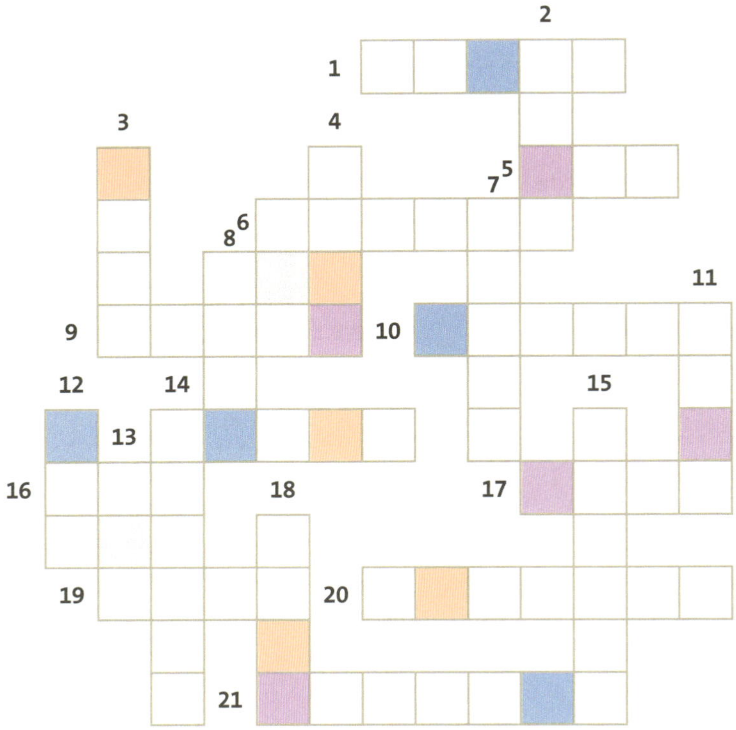

b) Use the letters …

1 in the **blue** boxes to write the simple past of choose: ______________

2 in the **purple** boxes to write the simple past of sleep: ______________

3 in the **orange** boxes to write the simple past of drink: ______________

9 LANGUAGE Questions for Mr Wu

Erklär-film

► SB, p. 22

Look at Mr Wu's answers. Then write the questions in the simple past.

1 When *did* __________ you *leave* __________ China? – I left China in 1972.

2 __________ you __________ much money back then? – No, we didn't have much money.

3 __________ that __________ you from coming to the USA? – No, it didn't stop us.

4 When __________ you __________ your business? – I started it many years ago.

5 __________ you __________ hard when you came here? – Yes, I did. I worked very hard.

6 How __________ you __________ when you first experienced racism? – I felt angry.

10 Language & Reading An interview about Lin-Manuel Miranda

▸ SB, p. 23

a) Look at the interview and write the verbs in the simple past. Remember that some verbs are irregular!

Q: Tell me about Lin-Manuel Miranda.

A: Well, he's a professional writer of songs and musicals. As a boy he (1) __________ (live) and (2) __________ (go) to school in a poor part of Manhattan with lots of people from South and Central America. His parents (3) __________ (come) to the US from Puerto Rico. They (4) __________ (meet) at college[1] in New York. His parents (5) __________ (not know) much English at first, so they (6) __________ (feel) comfortable in a neighbourhood where most people (7) __________ (speak) Spanish.

Q: When (8) __________ he __________ __________ (he / write) his first show for Broadway?

A: Oh, that (9) __________ (be) *In the Heights*, back in 2008. He (10) __________ (work) on the show when he (11) __________ (be) a student, and it (12) __________ (win) a lot of prizes on Broadway. But his show *Hamilton* is even more successful. Lin-Manuel (13) __________ only __________ __________ (not only / write) the musical, but he also (14) __________ (perform) in it for almost a year.

Q: I've heard that Lin-Manuel has done a lot to help Puerto Rico. Is that true?

A: Yes, it is. As a boy, he (15) __________ (spend) one month every year with his grandparents in Puerto Rico. In 2017 the island (16) __________ (have) a terrible hurricane[2], so Lin-Manuel and other artists (17) __________ (sing) his song *Almost like praying* and (18) __________ (give) the money that it (19) __________ (earn) to help the island.

b) Read the interview again and tick (✓) the three correct sentences.

1 Lin-Manuel lived in Puerto Rico when he was young. ☐
2 His parents went to college. ☐
3 No other family in the street spoke Spanish. ☐
4 He was an actor in his most famous show. ☐
5 He wrote *In The Heights* when he was still at school. ☐
6 He was often with his family in Puerto Rico when he was younger. ☐
7 Lin-Manuel used the money from his song *Almost like praying* for a holiday in Puerto Rico. ☐

[1] **college** *die Hochschule* [2] **hurricane** *der Hurrikan, der Orkan*

I can talk about diversity in New York City. ✓

11 READING American football

▸ Digital help ▸ SB, p. 25

a) Read the rules of American football. Then circle the correct words in sentences 1–6 below.

In some ways, American football is a bit like European football (or 'soccer') because there are eleven players in each team, and they try to score goals at the far end of the pitch. However, there are some important differences. For example, an American football isn't round, and players can pick the ball up with their hands and run with it. Also, there are two different ways to score a goal: kicking the ball between the goalposts (a 'field goal') or taking the ball to the end of the pitch (a 'touchdown').

Also, the game starts and stops a lot more often than in European football. Each team has four chances to move the ball to the next yard[1] line on the pitch. If they don't get the ball to the next line, then the other team gets four chances. The whole game takes one hour, with a break every fifteen minutes.

American footballers wear a helmet and special clothes to protect themselves because there is a lot of body contact: throwing another player to the ground is allowed. However, you are only allowed to do that to someone who has the ball in their hands.

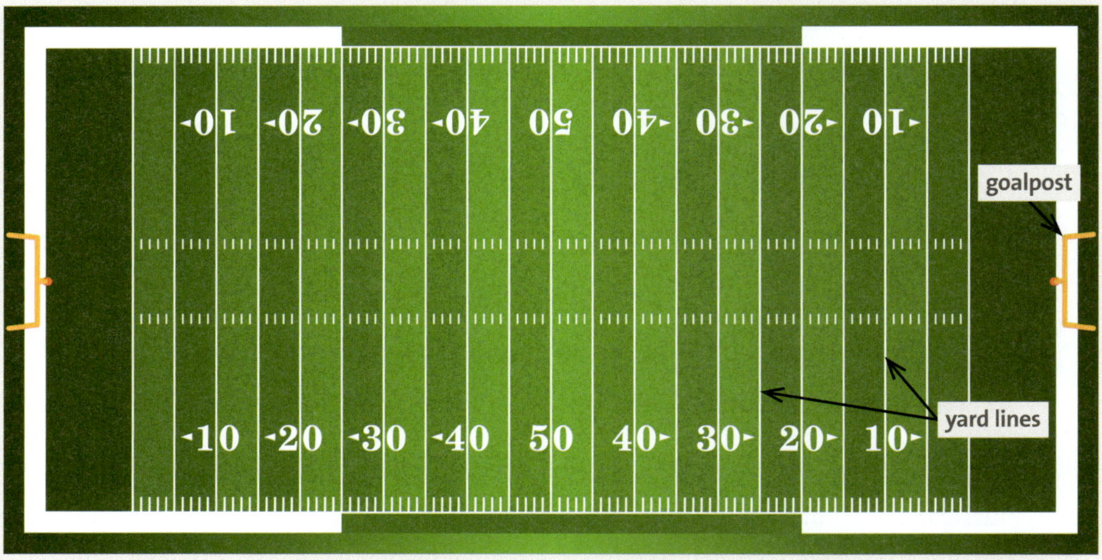

1 In American football, there can't / should be 11 players in a team.

2 Players mustn't / are allowed to run with the ball in their hands.

3 They can / have to score a goal by kicking the ball.

4 Each team must / shouldn't try to move the ball to the next line, or the other team will get the ball.

5 Players mustn't / have to wear special clothes to keep them safe.

6 Players can / mustn't throw other players to the ground, but they mustn't / must have body contact with players who don't have the ball.

b) Find and highlight three gerunds in the text.

c) 'Goalpost' is a new word. What do you think it means in German? ____________________

[1] **yard** *Längenmaß (= 91,44 cm)*

12 LANGUAGE Imani's basketball dreams

Erklär-film

▸ Digital help ▸ SB, p. 25

Read what Dante's friend Imani says. Then write the gerund of the verb in brackets.

1 I have always dreamed of becoming ______ (become) a famous basketball player one day.

2 I'm not super tall – but I AM fast and good at ______ (run)!

3 I practise ______ (throw) the ball every day after school and I'm getting better at ______ (score).

4 ______ (do) my best is important to me, and I'm not scared of ______ (work) hard to get where I want to be.

5 I find that ______ (watch) my favourite players on TV motivates me to try harder.

13 LANGUAGE My profile

▸ SB, p. 25

Use the ideas to help you, but remember to put the verbs into gerunds.
Example: I like swimming and going out with my friends.

1 *(swim / play ... / be with ... / go out with ... / ...)*
I like ______

2 *(eat ... / cycle / watch ... / ...)*
But I don't like ______

3 *(be kind / see ... / be with ... / do ... / ...)*
______ is something that's important to me.

4 *(go out late / walk across ... / ski down ... / climb ... / ...)*
I'm scared of ______

5 *(eat ... / do more ... / learn ... / ...)*
I want to start ______

6 *(win ... / sing in ... / run in ... / help ...)*
My proudest moment was ______
______

14 SPEAKING On the subway

► SB, p. 27

a) Partner B: Look at page 81.
Partner A: You want to use the subway in another city, but you don't understand the subway map. You're at Empire Station and want to get to 2nd Street. Ask your partner for help and write the information.

Excuse me, can you help me, please?
I don't really understand the map.
How can I get from ... to ...?

Take the __________ line to __________.

Change at __________.

Then take the __________ line.

b) Now look at the subway plan.
Listen to your partner and tell them the way.
Use the colours of the subway lines.

Take the ... line to ...
Change at ... Then take the ... line.

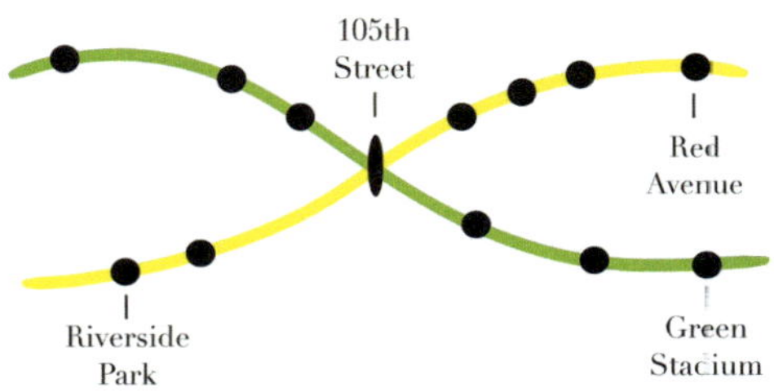

15 True and false friends

► Digital help ► SB, p. 27

a) Some English and German words look the same and mean the same. These are 'true friends', e.g. 'cowboy'. Can you think of at least four more 'true friends'?

1 __________ 2 __________ 3 __________ 4 __________

b) Some English and German words look the same, but mean different things. These are 'false friends'. Complete the table with words from the box. Then check in a dictionary.

Kunst • mutig • nett • nützlich • schlecht • werden

English	German
1 art	nicht Art oder Sorte, sondern __________
2 handy	nicht Telefon, sondern __________
3 bad	nichts mit Baden, sondern __________
4 brave	nicht brav, sondern __________
5 kind	nicht Kind, sondern __________
6 become	nicht bekommen, sondern __________

!
Be careful! False friends look like German words, but mean something different.

I can ask for and give help.

16 Questions about the story

► SB, p. 28–30

Answer the questions. Write what *you* think.

1 Why is Paul so tired? *Because he* ______.

2 Why is Paul annoyed with Ms Acosta? *Because he thinks* ______

______.

3 How does Paul feel when Emily smiles at him? *He feels* ______

______.

4 What are food-insecure families? *Families that* ______.

5 Why is Ms Henderson grateful? *Because Ms Acosta* ______

______.

17 A good teacher?

► SB, p. 28–30

Is Ms Acosta a good teacher? Why (not)?
Write what you think. Write at least 15–20 words.

I think Ms Acosta ______ *because* ______

______.

18 Global Goals Poverty in Germany

► SB, p. 28–30

Think about the problems Paul and his family have.
What problems do some people have in Germany and how can people help in your area?
Use the phrases and ideas in the boxes to help you.

not enough food
no place to live
can't buy things they need
can't pay for food

give money to charity
give food
volunteer for a charity
give blankets / tents / clothes

Some people in Germany don't have ______

People can ______

______

I can understand a text about poverty and dreams.

19 Directions

Write the directions[1].

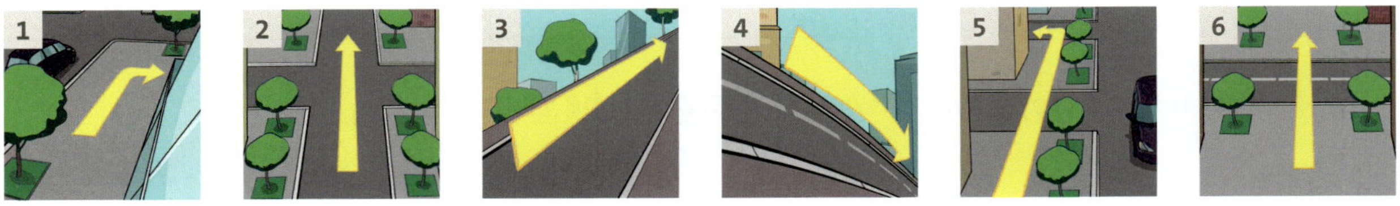

1 T______ r______.   2 Go s______ o______.   3 Go u______ the road.

4 Go d______ the road.   5 T______ the s______ road on the left.   6 C______ the road.

20 Asking the way

Complete the dialogue with the right words from the box.

along • excuse • for • have • help • how • on • third • welcome • your

Tourist	(1) ______ me, could you (2) ______ me, please?
	Could you tell me (3) ______ to get to Central Park?
New Yorker	Sure. Take the (4) ______ road on (5) ______ right.
	Go (6) ______ that road for a hundred meters. Then it's (7) ______ your left.
Tourist	Thanks (8) ______ your help.
New Yorker	You're (9) ______. (10) ______ a good day!

21 Words in the unit

a) Complete the puzzle with words in the unit.

1 A boat that always goes between the same two places.
2 The American word for 'toilet' is ...
3 A word that means 'really great'.
4 The money that you pay every month to the owner of your flat or house.
5 The part of you where your arm meets your body.
6 1.6 % = one ... six per cent
7 Male is for men and boys. This is the word for women and girls.

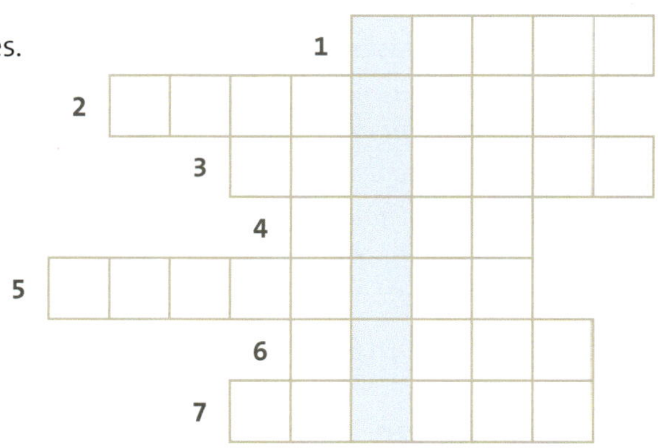

b) What's the word in blue?

______

[1] **directions** *die Wegbeschreibung(en)*

22 Definitions

Match words 1–6 to the correct definitions A–G. You don't need one definition.

1 chart ☐
2 war ☐
3 court ☐
4 seat ☐
5 shrug ☐
6 creator ☐

A when countries are fighting
B a place where you can sit
C move your shoulders up and down
D a diagram or table with information
E a person who makes something new
F the sound when air goes through your mouth
G a place where you can play tennis or basketball

23 American English words

Read the sentences. Circle seven American English words and write the British English words below them.

1 I took the subway into town. First I bought some sneakers and then I looked for some new pants.

underground

2 I'm trying to eat fewer cookies, candy and chips between meals.

____

3 Let's watch a movie. But first I need to go to the restroom.

____

24 Speaking Speak English well: American and British English

02 a) **Listen and read about two differences between American and British English.**

1 In American English, we say the R in these words. In British English, we don't.

certain – harbour – bird – of course

2 In American English, the T in these words is like D. In British English, it's a T.

water – city – pretty – writer

03 b) **Listen to eight speakers. Are they British (UK) or American (USA)? Circle the right answer,**

1 Do you like sports? USA / UK
2 Can I park my car here? USA / UK
3 Where were you born? USA / UK
4 It was hard to play on that court. USA / UK
5 I'm her daughter. USA / UK
6 Who is the creator of this art? USA / UK
7 I'm excited about visiting New York. USA / UK
8 That's not a crocodile. It's an alligator! USA / UK

In Unit 1, something interesting I learned about New York City was that

____

____

____

And something I learned about American English is that

____

____

____

My progress[1]

Read the *I can* statements and complete the sentences with the correct numbers for you.

1 I can talk about New York City.
2 I can present information about places in NYC.
3 I can talk about diversity in New York City.
4 I can ask for and give help.
5 I can understand a text about poverty and dreams.

I have made the most progress in statement(s) ______________ .

I haven't made as much progress yet in statement(s) ______________.

I found statement(s) ______________ the easiest.

I found statement(s) ______________ the hardest.

Every star shines a little differently.

My next steps

Highlight two *I can* statements that you want to improve and write two things you can do to help your progress for those statements.

I can ______________________________

____

I can ______________________________

____

[1] **progress** *der Fortschritt*

1 Joe's taxi puzzle

► Digital help

Joe is a taxi driver in NYC. Last week he only had one passenger[1] each day.
Each passenger went to a different place.
Read the sentences and work out which passengers Joe took to which place in NYC and on which day.
Use the grid[2] to help you.

1 Joe took Ha-Yoon to a green area, but not on Wednesday.

2 He took Kyle to a busy square on the second day of the week.

3 Paloma was Joe's last passenger, but she didn't go to Chinatown.

4 His first journey of the week was to Central Park.

5 He took Sita to a famous bridge on the day after Wednesday.

6 He went to the West Village on Friday, but he didn't take Viktor there.

	Times Square	Central Park	Chinatown	Brooklyn Bridge	West Village
Ha-Yoon	✗	✓	✗	✗	✗
Kyle		✗			
Paloma		✗			
Sita		✗			
Viktor		✗			

	Monday	Tuesday	Wednesday	Thursday	Friday
Ha-Yoon			✗		
Kyle					
Paloma					
Sita					
Viktor					

	place	day
Ha-Yoon	*Central Park*	
Kyle		
Paloma		
Sita		
Viktor		

► Check

[1] **passenger** *der Passagier, die Passagierin* [2] **grid** *das Raster*

1 Out and about in NYC

Erklär-film

**a) Write the verbs in the simple past.
The box on the right can help you.**

In the morning we (1) *visited* ______ (visit)

Central Park. We (2) ______ (sit) and

(3) ______ (watch) people playing tennis,

then we (4) ______ (walk) a bit and (5) ______ (buy) some pizza.

We (6) ______ (spend) about three hours in the park.

Remember

The simple past
1 Regular verbs in the simple past end in **-ed**:
play → **played**; phone → **phoned**
2 Irregular verbs change:
go → **went**; **see** → **saw**; **drink** → **drank**

b) Write the verbs in the simple past.

(1) *Did* ______ you *walk* ______ (walk)

along Broadway? And (2) ______ you

______ (see) any famous stars?

– No, we didn't … And we (3) ______ (not go in) to watch any show.

We (4) ______ (not want) to spend too much money.

Remember

For questions and negatives in the simple past use: **did/didn't** + **infinitive**
1 **Did** you **work** yesterday?
2 We **didn't go** there.

c) Complete the dialogue below with the verbs in the correct form of the simple past.

Amy (1) *Did* ______ you *take* ______ (take) the Staten Island Ferry?

Romy Yes, we did. And we (2) ______ (see) the Statue of Liberty. But we (3) *didn't* ______ ______ (not stay) on Staten Island. We (4) ______ (take) the first ferry back to Manhattan.

Amy (5) ______ you ______ (go up) one of the tall buildings in Manhattan?

Romy Yes, we did. But we (6) ______ (not go up) the Empire State Building. We (7) ______ (go up) the Rockefeller Building. That way we (8) ______ (have) a view of the Empire State Building.

Amy (9) ______ you ______ (use) the subway?

Romy Yes, we did. We (10) ______ (use) it to get to Fifth Avenue. But we (11) ______ (not get) a yellow taxi. We (12) ______ (want) to do that and then we (13) ______ (forget).

▸ Check

2 Do you know NYC?

Write the answers about New York City. Look at the pages in your book if you need help.

1 You can see this famous symbol of New York City from the Staten Island Ferry. *(p. 19)* ____________________

2 The Yankees and the Mets play this sport in New York. *(p. 24)* ____________________

3 The biggest park in New York City *(p. 18)* ____________________

4 The island where more than 12 million immigrants arrived between 1892 and 1924 *(p. 32)* ____________________

5 New York's second and third most popular languages after English *(p. 20)* ____________________

6 The highest building in New York *(p. 18)* ____________________

7 What New Yorkers call their underground trains *(p. 26)* ____________________

3 Do you know NYC?

a) **Complete the sentences with the right word from the box. You won't need all the words.**

asleep • grateful • homesick • public • ~~recommend~~ • rent • shrug • skip • used

1 We're looking for a good restaurant. Can you *recommend* one?

2 I ____________ my shoulders when I don't know the answer to a question.

3 On my first night away from home I felt a bit ____________ .

4 My uncle has a nice flat, but the ____________ is very high.

5 I was so tired when I came that I fell ____________ on the sofa.

6 I ____________ to come here when I was small.

7 I'm very ____________ to you for all the help you have given me.

b) **Find the partners and write the matching words.**

awesome • certain • commercial • exit • ~~female~~ • freedom • male • soccer

1 woman, girl *female*

2 liberty ____________

3 amazing ____________

4 sure ____________

5 advert ____________

6 man, boy ____________

7 way out ____________

8 football ____________

► Check

Unit 2
The South-East: Changing times

1 Viewing Nashville

▸ SB, p. 46

a) **Read the captions A–F below. Then watch the video. Put the places A–F in the order of the film. Write the numbers 1–6 in the boxes.**

A Hattie B's, a famous hot chicken restaurant ☐

B Nissan Stadium, where you can see American football ☐

C Broadway, Nashville's biggest street ☐

D Bridgestone Arena, where the Nashville hockey team plays ☐

E Printer's Alley, a cool street with lots of signs ☐

F A bus in Nashville – a good place to have a party ☐

b) **Watch the video again and circle the correct information.**

1 In Broadway you hear the music from restaurants through open doors / windows.

2 The *Matriarchs* are K's band / baseball team.

3 When you buy a pair of boots in the boot store you get one free pair / two free pairs of boots.

4 K says the Batman Building is a big Nashville store / looks like Batman.

5 At Hattie B's there's a line of people at the weekends / every day.

6 The *Tennessee Titans* play hockey / American football.

c) **Do you think you would like to visit Nashville? Complete one answer.**

Yes, because I like ______________________________

______________________________________.

Or:

No, because I prefer ______________________________

______________________________________.

2 The South-East of the USA

► SB, p. 47

a) Write the names of the places. Check your answers on pages 46–47 of your book.

1 This long river is the M i s s i s s i p p i.

2 N _ _ _ _ _ _ _ _ is famous for its country and rock music.

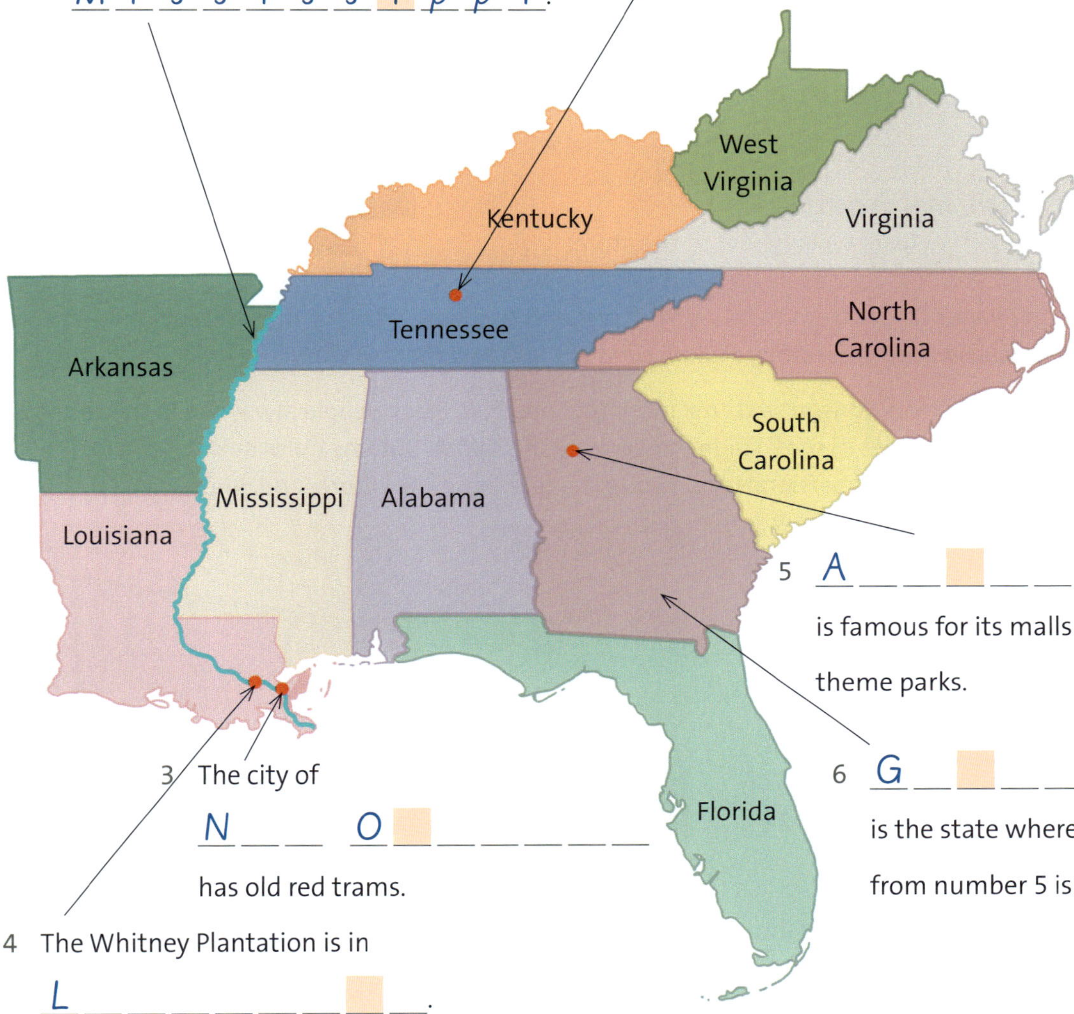

3 The city of N _ _ O _ _ _ _ _ _ has old red trams.

4 The Whitney Plantation is in L _ _ _ _ _ _ _ _.

5 A _ _ _ _ _ _ is famous for its malls and theme parks.

6 G _ _ _ _ _ _ is the state where the city from number 5 is the capital.

b) Use the letters in orange to complete the name. The map on page 47 will help you.

Columbia is the capital city of South C _ _ _ _ _ _ _.

3 What's in the pictures?

► SB, p. 47

Write the letter A–F of the pictures in your book on pages 46–47 with ...

1 a boat ____ 2 trees ____ 3 tall modern buildings ____

4 the US flag ____ 5 a small simple house ____ 6 somebody's back ____

7 a singer ____

I can talk about the South-East of the USA.

4 READING Rosie's post

▶ SB, p. 48

a) **Read Rosie's post and look at the pictures. Then answer the questions.**

Last vacation I was with my friend Mason in a mall in Atlanta and we went into a store to buy some candy. 'Do you want the receipt?' the woman asked when we paid for them, and Mason and I both answered together.
'No, thanks,' I said.
'Yes, please,' Mason said.
Then, when we were walking out of the store, I laughed and said to Mason, 'Why do ask for a receipt? Paper comes from trees, right? If we all stop taking receipts, that will save a lot of trees.'
Mason's answer surprised me. He looked at me and told me this story:

'When I was small,' Mason said, 'my mom told me, "We Black people always keep the receipts. Always. Never forget it, son." I didn't know *why* she said it. But, my mom said it, so I did it. And then one day two white friends and I bought a few things in a store, and when we came out of the store some security guards stopped us.

"Did you pay for those things?" they asked.
"Sure thing," we all said.
"You," one of the guards then said to me. "Open your bag."
And she looked in my bag. Only my bag, not my friends' bags. And my friends didn't say anything.
"Lots of nice things here," she said. "Did you steal them?"
And suddenly I understood why my mom had said we must always keep the receipts.
"I paid for them," I answered. "And I have the receipt."
When I showed it to her, she and the other guards left us.
So, you see, Rosie, that's why I always ask for a receipt.'

I felt terrible. And ashamed.
You see, I'm a white kid from a white neighborhood. We never have any trouble with security guards. And I thought I knew about the world – you know, I read the news, we discuss things at home.

But a receipt showed me that I knew nothing about the life of other kids in my own school.

1 Who had a problem? ______________________ 2 Who was racist? ______________________

b) **Read the sentences below. Are they true (T) or false (F)?**

1 Rosie and Mason bought candy in a mall. ☐
2 In the store, Rosie and Mason both asked for a receipt. ☐
3 Rosie could not understand why Mason asked for a receipt. ☐
4 Rosie wants to use less paper and save trees. ☐
5 In his story, Mason was with some friends. ☐
6 Security guards came into the store while Mason and his friends were shopping. ☐
7 The security guards looked through the bags of Mason and his friends. ☐
8 Rosie learns that Mason keeps receipts to show he hasn't stolen anything. ☐

c) **Look in the text and find the American English words for the following words.**

1 holiday ___________ 2 shopping centre _________ 3 sweets _______ 4 shop ____________

Erklär-film

5 Language When Rosie and Mason go shopping …

► SB, p. 49

Look at the modal verbs in blue. Then circle the correct modal verb in each sentence.

1 Rosie and Mason like shopping malls because they can / must buy different things in one place.
They needn't / aren't allowed to go to lots of different places.
But smaller shops may / must sometimes be more interesting.

2 When Rosie and Mason buy things in a shop, they have to / needn't pay for them.
If they can't / mustn't pay by cash, they must / mustn't worry.
In almost all shops you may / must pay by card.

3 Rosie needn't / mustn't worry about receipts.
But Mason must / mustn't always keep his receipts because security guards might / have to think he has stolen things from a shop.
With a receipt, he is able to / allowed to show that he has paid for everything.

4 Security guards are allowed to / have to look in people's bags.
But they have to / needn't to be fair.
They mustn't / might look in people's bags just because they are Black.

I can talk about rules.

6 Listening My favourite movie

▶ SB, p. 50

04

a) Read the sentences below. Then listen to a podcast about *Hidden Figures*, a film about Black women at NASA, the American space organization. Tick (✓) the correct answer A, B or C.

1 Yuri Gagarin was ...
- A the first woman in space. ☐
- B the first American in space. ☐
- C the first man in space. ☐

2 Elias says the people in the space movies ...
- A were all men. ☐
- B were all white. ☐
- C were all scientists. ☐

3 We've never heard about the Black people at NASA because ...
- A there weren't any. ☐
- B they weren't important. ☐
- C nobody told their story. ☐

4 Computers in the 1960s were ...
- A people, not machines. ☐
- B smaller than computers today. ☐
- C able to do maths but nothing else. ☐

5 Katherine Johnson ...
- A worked in an office of white men. ☐
- B didn't like men. ☐
- C was the first Black woman in space. ☐

6 Mae Jemison became the first Black American woman in space ...
- A in 1987. ☐
- B in 1990. ☐
- C in 1992. ☐

b) Mediation Your dad listens to the podcast, but doesn't understand the part about Katherine Johnson and the toilet. Answer his questions in German.

1 Warum durfte Katherine nicht dieselben Toiletten benutzen wie ihre Kollegen?

Damals gab es bei der NASA ______________________

____

____

2 Wie weit weg war die Toilette, die Katherine benutzen durfte?

____

____

Katherine Johnson

3 Warum sagten Katherines Kollegen sie sei faul?

____

____

☒ 7 READING The story of Rosa Parks

▸ SB, p. 50

Read the text and then answer the questions.

Rosa Parks

In December 1955, in Montgomery, Alabama, a Black woman called Rosa Parks got on a bus and sat down in the seats for Black people. But there weren't enough seats for white people, and the law in Alabama said that if there weren't enough seats for everybody, Black people had to give their seats to white people. But Rosa Parks didn't do that. When the driver told her to move, she stayed in her seat. So the driver called the police and the police threw Rosa off the bus. But the Black people were so angry about this that they stopped using the buses. They walked to work, and they walked home again ... for 381 days! The buses then lost so much money that Alabama had to change the law and Black people didn't have to give their seats to white people any more.

1 How did Rosa Parks break the law? ____________________

2 How did the Black people protest? ____________________

3 Who was violent in this story? ____________________

4 Who was racist in this story? ____________________

8 LANGUAGE Modal verbs

▸ SB, p. 51

Look at what Black people said and then write about the life of Black people in 1955. Use the words from the box.

had to (2x) • was allowed to • were able to • weren't able to • weren't allowed to

1 "We can't sit when white people have no seats." — Back in 1955, Black people ____________ sit when white people had no seats.

2 "We must stand up so that the white people can sit." — Black people ____________ stand up so that the white people ____________ sit.

3 "A police officer can throw us off the bus if we don't stand up." — A police officer ____________ throw a Black person off the bus if they didn't stand up.

4 "Now we don't use the bus, and the buses can't make any money." — But Black people didn't use the bus, and the buses ____________ make any money.

5 "This law must change!" — And the law about standing up in buses ____________ change.

I can talk about justice.

9 MEDIATION The Jambalaya Festival

► SB, p. 55

A neighbour who likes cooking and is planning a holiday in the USA has found this information online. Read the information and answer his questions in German.

1 Wie oft findet das Festival statt?

____

____

2 Was waren die beiden Ziele des Festivalgründers?

____

____

____

3 Wie muss Jambalaya gekocht werden?

____

____

____

4 Tausende von Gästen kommen zum Festival. Was sind zwei weitere Zeichen dafür, dass dieses Festival erfolgreich ist?

____

____

____

5 Wann findet das Festival statt?

____

____

____

6 Welche Aktivitäten waren im Jahr 1971 neu?

____

____

____

The Jambalaya Festival

Gonzales is a small town in Louisiana, not a famous town. Most people in the South-East of the USA have never heard of it.

In 1967, Steve Juneau had an idea.

"More visitors will come to Gonzales," he thought, "if we organize a Jambalaya Festival every year. And the festival can also make money for community projects."

Jambalaya is a really typical Louisiana dish which you make with chicken and rice.

In the first festival in 1968, 13 cooks were in competition to be the 'World Jambalaya Cooking Champion'. In 1971, 50,000 visitors came to the festival, and there were 16 cooks. The rules aren't easy. Each cook gets some rice, chicken, vegetables and spices and they must cook their jambalaya over an open fire.

The competition has become bigger and now each year about 70 cooks try to win the world title at the festival, which takes place on Memorial Day weekend, which is the last weekend in May.

In 1971, there was a horse race[1] and an art show, and now there are different activities each year like boxing competitions, car shows, five-kilometer runs, story-telling, singing, bike races, bed races, dances and baseball, tennis and golf tournaments.

[1] **horse race** *Pferderennen*

10 Speaking How to make jambalaya

► SB, p. 55

Partner B: Look at page 82.

Partner A: You and your partner have different copies of the recipe. Take turns to

- ask a question and write the missing information in the recipe.
- listen to your partner and give the missing information.

You ask the first question.

Note: Don't read everything – just give your partner the missing information.

How to make jambalaya

A

frying pan with lid

B

chicken stock

C

celery

D

garlic

E

cajun seasoning

F

green pepper

1 *I have the celery, the green pepper and the tomato. What other vegetables do I need?*

2 *Answer your partner's question: Fry it …*

3 *What do I have to do when the chicken is brown?*

4 *Answer your partner's question: You …*

5 *How long do I have to fry the vegetables?*

6 *Answer your partner's question: You …*

7 *OK, my, chicken stock is really hot. What do I do now?*

8 *Answer your partner's question: You …*

1 **You will need:**
- a frying pan with a lid
- chicken, sausage, chicken stock[1]
- celery, a green pepper, a tomato and ____________
- garlic, spices and cajun seasoning
- rice, some oil[2], flour, salt and pepper

2 Put some oil in a large frying pan. Fry the chicken till both sides are brown.

3 When the chicken is brown, ______________________

______________________________________.

4 Now fry both sides of the sausage, then put it on the dish with the chicken.

5 Add some flour to the frying pan and mix well. Add the onion, garlic, celery, green peppers and fry for ______________________

______________________________________.

6 Cut the tomato in small pieces and put it in the frying pan with salt, pepper, spices and cajun seasoning. Mix well.

7 Add the chicken stock and the rice. When the stock is really hot, add ______________________

______________________________________.

8 Put a lid on the frying pan and cook for twenty minutes.

And that's it. Enjoy!

[1] **chicken stock** *die Geflügelbrühe* [2] **oil** *das Öl*

11 Language Opinions about music

▸ Digital help ▸ SB, p. 56

Complete the sentences with adverbs from the box. Use each adverb only once.

a little • extremely • mostly • not very • really • too

1 I love music, that is ____________ important to me.

2 What do you think of this band? – Well, no, they're ____________ good.

3 Do you like American music? – Some of it. I ____________ listen to rock music.

4 Sorry, now I can't hear you! The music is ____________ loud.

5 Wow, you play the trumpet ____________ well! You should give a concert!

– I'd like to, but I'm ____________ shy.

12 A festival

▸ Digital help ▸ SB, p. 56

a) **Choose a festival and complete the mind map with as many words as you can.**
Some ideas: ***play, wear, drink, invite, give, decorate, sing, we don't ... in our family, ...***

food

____
____
____
____

music

____
____
____
____

My festival: ____________________

people

____
____
____
____

activities

____
____
____
____

b) **Find two partners and look at their mind maps. Can you find some ideas to add to your mind map?**

c) Writing **Use your mind map to write a short text to recommend your festival in your exercise book.**

I can **make recommendations.**

13 VIEWING Storm chasers

► SB, p. 61

a) **Can you remember? Circle the correct words from the video.**

1 The storm chasers have found very large hailstones / floods.

2 As storm chasers, Dick and Reed give warnings about / follow the storm.

3 They're driving across Oklahoma / Alabama to get a better look at one of the largest tornadoes they have ever seen.

4 It's hard to know / choose the best road to take.

5 Reed wants to drive past / into the tornado.

6 He calls the local television weather channel / news programme.

7 When the rain / wind starts to break the car, it's time to go home.

8 That was one of the most dangerous / amazing tornadoes I've ever seen.

b) **Now watch the video again and check.**

14 WRITING An interview about you and extreme weather

► SB, p. 61

Answer the questions about a time when you experienced extreme weather.

1 Where were you when this happened?

____

2 What type of extreme weather was it?

____

3 Did the weather suddenly change? How?

____

4 And what happened when the bad weather hit you?

____

5 How did you feel after this happened?

____

____

15 Crossword

a) **Complete the crossword puzzle.**

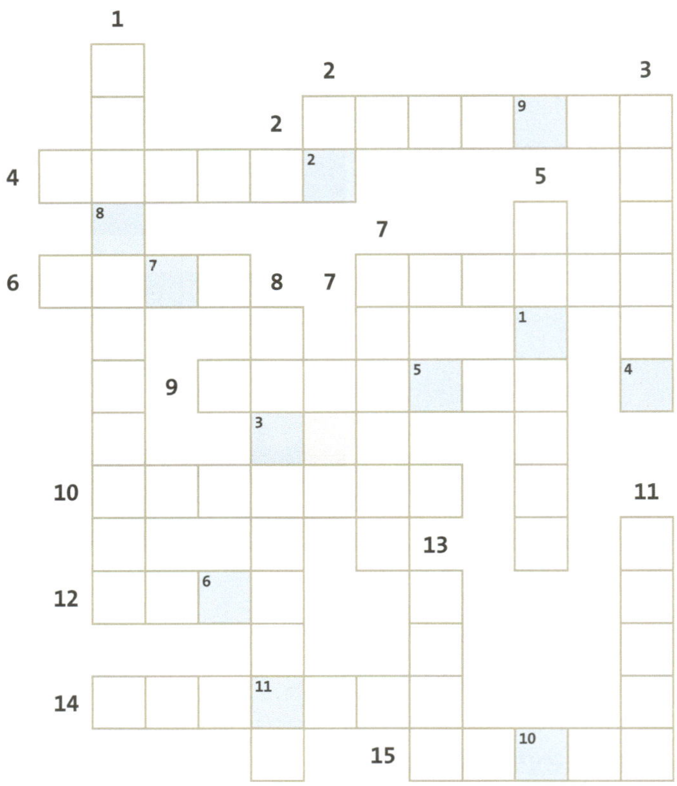

1 you play music on them
2 *(across)* from the verb warn: you give this when you know something dangerous is going to happen
2 *(down)* you and I
3 collect, e.g. information
4 get away from someone who will not allow you to leave
5 the opposite of build
6 a small train that runs on streets in town
7 *(across)* Martin Luther King gave a famous … with the words: "I have a dream."
7 *(down)* completely quiet
8 In a thunder storm, the sky is sometimes white with …
9 the opposite of peaceful
10 not anything
11 make a new building
12 write your name on a document
13 the top of a house or building
14 a very, very strong wind, e.g. in the USA
15 when river water comes into fields and houses

b) **Use the letters in blue to write the correct word.**

The system in the South-East of the USA till the 1960s, when Black and white people had to live separately and Black and white children couldn't learn together, was called:

1	2	3	4	5	6	7	8	9	10	11

16 Small words

Write the correct word from the box in each sentence.

as • at • for • in • of (2x) • over • since • to • up

1 I need a cup ________ tea.

2 We have lived here ________ 2018.

3 There's a chair ________ the back of the room.

4 I like fruit, ________ example apples.

5 We went home when the game was ________.

6 She reacted ________ his words with a smile.

7 Come and visit us ________ soon as you can.

8 I'll be an athlete when I grow ________.

9 This spoon is made ________ plastic.

10 There was a lot of racism ________ the 1960s.

17 Focus on verbs

Complete each sentence with the correct blue verbs.

1 It was a great hotel. The people *treated* us very well and the price ________ breakfast and our evening meal. (included / treated)

2 The terrible storm ________ all night, so in the morning we ________ on our neighbour, to see if he was OK. (blew / checked)

3 Every night, when I ________ up, my mum ________ next to my bed and ________ me goodnight. (grew / kissed / knelt)

4 A man came into my house, ________ my notepad and ________ through the window. But the police ________ him down the street and ________ him. (caught / chased / escaped / stole)

18 SPEAKING Speak English well: [ə] in unstressed[1] syllables[2]

05

a) **The sound [ə] is called *schwa*. In English, we say a schwa in many unstressed syllables. Listen to these examples and repeat the words.**

1 A • me • ri • ca [əˈmerɪkə] 2 Eng • land [ˈɪŋɡlənd] 3 hu • man [ˈhjuːmən]

b) **Highlight the schwa sounds in the following words.**

1 viral
2 stolen
3 continue
4 funeral
5 behaviour
6 violent

06

c) **Listen and check your answers.**

d) **Now read the six words to your partner.**

[1] **unstressed** *unbetont* [2] **syllable** *die Silbe*

In Unit 2, I learned about ______________________________

____

I know ...

- the names of some cities in the South-East of the USA: ______________________________

  ____
- some American English words: ______________________________
- some useful words to talk about racism: ______________________________

  ____
- extreme weather words: ______________________________

I can ...

- use modal verbs: *I can play the trumpet. You* ______________________________

  ____
- use *must, must not* and *can* in the past tense: *Rosa Parks had to stand up, she* ______________________________

  ____
- use adverbs of degree: *It isn't very warm. / I'm* ______________________________

  ____

My progress[1]

Tick (✓) what you enjoy in English and put an (✗) for what you find hard in English.

- ☐ practising my spoken English
- ☐ listening to English
- ☐ learning about life in the USA
- ☐ talking about topics like racism
- ☐ talking about difficult topics
- ☐ learning new words
- ☐ remembering words
- ☐ writing English
- ☐ understanding people when they speak English

[1] **progress** *der Fortschritt*

1 Words about racism

Find one word in each line of the wordsearch. Then use the ten words in sentences 1–5 below.

D	I	S	C	R	I	M	I	N	A	T	I	O	N
F	R	U	P	E	A	V	I	O	L	E	N	T	S
L	J	U	S	T	I	C	E	P	U	R	I	U	H
I	G	S	R	A	I	Y	S	H	O	C	K	E	D
B	H	P	J	P	E	A	C	E	F	U	L	G	C
P	E	T	I	T	I	O	N	I	I	O	E	O	K
O	S	E	G	R	E	G	A	T	I	O	N	R	E
G	O	K	A	Z	S	L	A	V	E	R	Y	N	D
A	O	I	N	J	U	S	T	I	C	E	N	O	T
F	T	P	V	L	A	W	Y	N	R	A	R	P	Y

1 ________________ is when there are different schools for Black and white children, for example.

2 In the 1960s, the police were often ________________ against ________________ people in the streets.

3 The ________________ should help people to get ________________.

4 Boats brought African people to America as slaves. I was ________________ when I learned about ________________. It was a terrible ________________ against Black people.

5 Please sign this ________________ against ________________ against all kinds of people.

▸ Check

2 A wordsearch with words about food

▸ Digital help

Write eight food words in the wordsearch, then fill the other spaces with other letters. Then show your wordsearch to a partner. Can they find your eight words?

										S												
										W												
										E												
										E												
										T												

1 The Everglades National Park in Florida

Erklär-film

a) Read the rules of the Everglades National Park. Circle the right verb.

1 You must / might meet a wild animal in the park.

2 Remember: You aren't able / aren't allowed to give food to the wild animals.

3 It gets very hot, so you should / mustn't bring some drinking water with you.

4 Pets can scare the wild animals, so you don't have to / mustn't bring dogs into the park.

5 The park can be a dangerous place. Parents must / can make sure their children are safe.

6 You mustn't / needn't leave any rubbish in the park.

7 You mustn't / needn't leave the park in the evening – there are two places where you can camp.

b) Replace the verbs in blue with the right forms of *able to / allowed to / have to / don't have to.*

1 Must I pay to go into the park?

Do ________ I ________ pay to go into the park?

2 Can you see all the park in one day?

________ you ________ see all the park in one day?

3 You needn't pay by cash. You ________ pay by cash.

4 You can't make a fire in the park. You ________ make a fire in the park.

c) Complete the questions with *able to / allowed to / have to* in the simple past.

When you went to the Everglades last month ...

1 Were ________ you ________ camp in the park or was that against the rules?

2 ________ you ________ wait long to go in?

3 ________ you ________ see any alligators?

d) Write the sentences. Use a modal verb: *must / mustn't / should / shouldn't*.

1 make / lot / noise / park

You ________________________________.

2 treat / plants / animals / respect

You ________________________________.

▸ Check

2 A review of a place to eat

Complete the text with words from the box.

amazing • don't • if • miss • out • recommend

(1) ______________ you're a fan of good food, you'll love *Pete's Eatery*. I can really (2) ______________ it. It's a friendly place and the food is great. Above all, don't (3) ______________ the desserts – they're (4) ______________. You really should check this place (5) ______________. But (6) ______________ forget that it's closed on Mondays!

3 New words in Unit 2

a) **Write the words in the right lists.**

~~cup~~ • dangerous • discrimination • hail • hurricane • lightning • peaceful • polite • racism • receipt • segregation • slavery • spoon • strange • thunder • tornado • toy • trumpet • violent • violin

you can take it in your hand	injustice	weather	behaviour
cup			

b) **Write the opposites.**

1 build ↔ *d* _ _ _ _ _ *y*

2 everything ↔ *n* _ _ _ _ _ *g*

3 stop an activity ↔ *c* _ _ _ _ _ _ *e*

c) **Write words that mean the same.**

1 run away – *e* _ _ _ _ *e*

2 quiet – *s* _ _ _ _ *t*

3 take without paying – *s* _ _ _ *l*

► Check

Unit 3
Texas: Teen life

1 Reading Texan cowboy culture

► SB, p. 77

a) Before Reading Look at the photo in the online article and make notes about what you can see. How does it make you feel?

I can see ________________________________

The photo makes me feel ________________________________

b) Read the online article and tick (✓) the three correct sentences below.

www.texas-rodeos.example.com

Fun or just mean to animals?

Traditional rodeos are a popular activity in Texas. Rodeos are big events with concerts, parades, food stalls and shopping. The biggest rodeo in Houston, Texas, is three weeks long, and thousands of people go to watch cowboys and cowgirls in competitions.

There are about 1,000 rodeos every year in the USA. But only about six hundred rodeos follow the rules of a professional organization which tries to protect the animals. Many people think that isn't enough and say rodeos are bad for animals, and that there should be no more rodeos. Riders[1] can give horses electric shocks. This hurts the horses, of course, and makes them angrier and 'more fun' to watch.

However, others, like Cassidy, a professional cowgirl from Austin, think the opposite. 'We do our best to look after the horses. I don't think we should stop rodeos because they have always been an important part of Texan culture. They bring people together and also create jobs,' she says.

What do you think? Traditional fun or mean to the animals? Let us know in the comments!

1 Rodeos have been banned in Texas. ☐
2 The rodeo in the text is fourteen days long. ☐
3 The article talks about people who ride cows. ☐
4 Today, all rodeos protect the animals. ☐
5 Some people think we need to do more to help the animals in rodeos. ☐
6 Some riders hurt the horses to make them angry and move around more. ☐

[1] **rider** *der Reiter, die Reiterin*

I can talk about Texas. ✓

07

2 LISTENING Fredericksburg statistics

▶ SB, p. 78

Listen to the radio show and complete the table.

Remember to use commas in English to show thousands.
1,000 = one thousand *(German: 1.000 = eintausend)*

Built in: ____________

Population: ____________

Location: ______ miles west of Austin

Enchanted Rock: ____________ feet high

Number of Texas German speakers: ____________

Enchanted Rock

3 Small towns and big cities

Erklär-film

▶ SB, p. 79

a) Match the two parts of the sentences.

1 If you don't want to cook, [E]
2 If you don't have a car, [ ]
3 If you go to the centre, [ ]
4 If you're a young person, [ ]
5 If you have a problem, [ ]
6 If you want to live in an apartment here, [ ]

A you won't find much to do here.
B it will probably be quite expensive.
C you'll find it difficult to travel around.
D one of your neighbours will help you.
E you'll find lots of restaurants here.
F there will be lots of air pollution because of the traffic.

b) Highlight the sentences in a) that are about small towns.
Which sentences could be about both small towns and big cities? ____________

c) Now write the sentences with the words in the right order.

1 you / in a small town / live — know / you'll / all your neighbours

If ____

2 live / you / in a city — there / lots of shops / will be

If ____

Remember

Mit Bedingungssätzen vom Typ 1 sagst du, was unter bestimmten Bedingungen passieren wird. Es ist durchaus möglich, dass die Bedingung erfüllt wird.

If it **rains** tomorrow,	I'**ll take** the bus.
if + **present tense**	**will-future**

4 Reading **Where should you live?**

► SB, p. 81

a) Read the quiz cards (1–5) and circle your answers.

1 If I designed my perfect home, it would be a ...
- A beautiful big apartment on the top floor.
- B a big house with trees all around.
- C flat in a nice house with a garden close to the stores.

2 If my neighbors knew everything about me, I'd ...
- A hate it – I need space!
- B love it – I like talking to people!
- C move as far away from them as possible.

3 If I described my perfect neighborhood in one word, it would be ...
- A exciting.
- B friendly.
- C quiet.

4 I'd be happiest at home if I had ...
- A lots of fun things to do in the area.
- B my friends near me.
- C nature all around me.

5 I'd hate it most if ...
- A there weren't any cool stores.
- B I didn't know anyone in the area.
- C there were too many cars.

b) Look at the answers on page 53 in your workbook and write your reaction.

► WB, p. 53

The quiz says I should live ____________________

I agree / don't agree because ____________________

____

____

Erklär-film

c) Look at the sentences in a). Then circle the correct answers in the tip box.

In Bedingungssätzen vom Typ 2 ist es **sehr wahrscheinlich / möglich, aber unwahrscheinlich**, dass die Bedingung erfüllt wird.

If I **go / went** to Texas, I **wouldn't / won't** go and watch a rodeo.
if + **present / past tense** verb with **would / will**

5 LANGUAGE Texas and you

► SB, p. 81

Write the sentences with the words in the right order.

1 I / Fredericksburg / visited → would speak / I / German.

______

2 Texan students / to my school / came → would be / they / very surprised

______

6 LANGUAGE Chain sentences

► SB, p. 81

Write the correct form of the verbs in brackets to complete the chain sentences.

1 If I ______ (live) in America, I *would learn* (learn) to drive at 16.

2 If I *learned* (learn) to drive at 16, I ______ (want) my own car.

3 If I ______ (want) my own car, I ______ (need) money to buy one.

4 If I ______ (need) money to buy my own car, I ______ (get) a Saturday job.

5 If I ______ (get) a Saturday job, I *wouldn't* (not need) pocket money from my parents.

6 If I *didn't* (not need) pocket money from my parents, I ______ (not ask) them for it.

7 Funny situations

► SB, p. 81

a) **Write two funny if-clauses. Use two of the ideas from the box below or your own ideas and complete them with *would / wouldn't + verb*.**

If I met Taylor Swift on my way to school, ... • If I still had my slippers on when I arrived at school, ... • If NASA gave me a place on a mission to Mars, ...

1 *If* ______

______

2 *If* ______

______

b) **Now read your sentences to your partner. Can you make her/him laugh?**

I can talk and write about small-town life.

8 WORDS American schools

▸ SB, p. 82

electives • freshmen • grades • guns • Pledge • prom • senior • sophomore

Complete the captions with the correct words.

1 

I'm in the first year of high school, so I'm a ____________. My brother is in the year above, so he's a ____________.

2 

Soon the ____________ students – the ones in the last year of school – will have a really cool party called ____________!

3 

Some colleges have security guards to check students aren't carrying kives or ____________.

4 

This is my class standing for the ____________ of Allegiance to the flag.

5 

I really like geography, but I don't have very good ____________ in that.

6 

Students can choose their own activities in classes called ____________.

9 School stresses and positives

▸ Digital help ▸ SB, p. 82

a) Complete the table. Use six ideas from the box and some of your own ideas if you want to.

being popular at school • break time • bullying • exams • food at school • friends • grades • homework • lessons • school clothes • school clubs • teachers • travelling to school

stressful ☹	fun ☺

b) Compare with a partner. Do you have the same opinions?

I find exams stressful. What about you?

Yes, me too.

Oh, they're not so bad.

10 READING A question and three ideas

▸ SB, p. 84

a) Read the social media post and the comments. What are they about?

____

Guys, I need your help!!! 🙏🙏🙏
I don't want to wait for my boyfriend to ask me to prom – I want to ask him! But I can't think of a cool way to do it. Do you have any ideas? What great prom invitations have you seen? – Phoebe10

A friend in my class had a really cute idea for a prom invitation! He's an amazing baker, so he made a box of cupcakes and brought them to class. 🙏 He offered me a cake first and when I opened the box, I saw 'Prom?' written on the cakes! Of course, I said yes! 🍟 (And the cakes were delicious too!) – Unicorns4eva

Aww, I love that idea! My boyfriend did a really sweet idea for a prom invitation too last year. I'm on the school baseball team, and the school band always plays before the game. He asked them to play my favourite song and then he came onto the pitch with a microphone and sang to me, then asked me to prom! 😳 I was kind of embarrassed, but it was also cute! ❤️ – James_R

Well, I don't really understand why everyone has to do these big prom invitations. I'm pretty shy and I would hate someone to ask me to prom in front of the whole school! There's a girl in my class that I really like, but I don't know if she would want to go to prom with me. If I feel brave enough to ask her – and that's a big IF – then I'll just write a letter and leave it on her desk before class. That way, if she says no, I don't have to see her laughing at me. 😭 – LonghornsFan

b) Read the text again and match the sentences to the writers (Phoebe10, Unicorns4eva, James_R or LonghornsFan).

1 This person's boyfriend asked them to prom. ______________

2 This person isn't sure if they want to ask someone to prom or not. ______________

3 This person doesn't know how to ask someone to prom. ______________

4 This person talks about a musical prom invitation. ______________

5 This person talks about a prom invitation made in food. ______________

6 This person doesn't think everyone should see their prom invitation. ______________

c) Write your idea for a good prom invitation in your exercise book and then compare with a partner.

write	a poem / a letter / a song / the word 'Prom?' on ... / ...
organize	a big prom invitation in front of everyone / a song and dance / something with friends / ...
make	a big poster and put it ... / a special box with ... inside / a T-shirt with ... on it / ...
give him / her	some flowers / a present / a balloon / ...
ask him / her	quietly / at lunch time / during a ... match / during class / ...

11 LISTENING Nina and her mom

08

► SB, p. 85

a) Diego's sister Nina is a senior at college. Listen to her talking with her mum. What are they talking about?

____

b) Listen again and circle the correct answers.

1 Nina hasn't bought her earrings / shoes for prom, yet.
2 She's going to buy them online / downtown.
3 When Nina says her mom lived in the 1890s it's a joke / she's being mean.
4 Nina's parents / Nina and her friends are going to pay for the car.
5 At prom, Nina is going to write a poem / messages in her friends' yearbooks.
6 At the end, Nina feels really excited / a bit sad.

c) Look at Nina's yearbook page and label the different parts.

- class name
- message
- name
- photo

d) How do students celebrate when they leave your school? Write at least three sentences.

On the last day of school	we (don't)	have a party / barbecue / yearbook / ...
At my school		wear nice clothes / smart clothes / costumes / ...
		bring party food / drink / games / family / music / ...
		take photos / write messages / say goodbye / sing songs / ...

____

____

____

____

____

I can describe school life in the USA.

12 What I would do if ...

► SB, p. 86

Match the two parts of the sentences.

1 If I wanted to work with small children, I ...	B	A would go to university.
2 If I wanted to speak English better, I ...		B would first go to a vocational school.
3 If I wanted to help people, I ...		C would get a job.
4 If I wanted to study to become a doctor, I ...		D would do an apprenticeship.
5 If I wanted to earn money straight away, I ...		E would live in an English-speaking country.
6 If I wanted to learn how to become a mechanic and also earn money, I ...		F would do volunteer work.

13 MEDIATION An advert

► SB, p. 87

You've found this advert in your local town and you are interested in it. Tell an English exchange student in your class about it. Answer their questions in English.

1 What is the advert offering?

____

2 Are they looking for a boy?

____

3 When would you work?

____

____

4 How much money would you earn?

____

5 How old do you need to be?

____

6 What kind of person are they looking for?

____

____

____

Hundesitter/in gesucht!

Du liebst Hunde? Du hast diesen Sommer Zeit? Wir suchen für die Sommerferien Hundesitter/innen in der näheren Umgebung.

Was wir bieten:
- Flexible Arbeitszeiten: je nach Verfügbarkeit kannst du wählen, wie viele Tage du arbeiten möchtest
- 9 EUR pro Stunde
- Komplette Ausrüstung wird zur Verfügung gestellt

Anforderungen:
- Du musst mindestens vierzehn Jahre alt sein.
- Du musst zuverlässig und gut im Umgang mit Hunden sein.
- Du musst im Juli und August mindestens einen Tag pro Woche arbeiten können.

Interessiert? Dann schreib uns per E-Mail, warum du die ideale Person bist. Wir freuen uns auf deine Bewerbung!

14 Jobs puzzle

► SB, p. 87

a) **Read the sentences and complete the puzzle with the answers in the boxes.**

babysitter *dog walker*[1] *shop assistant* *waiter*	*$15* *$17* *$19* *$20*	*Thursdays* *Fridays* *Saturdays* *Sundays*

1 Sami looks after his neighbour's daughter on the last day of the week.

2 Wei earns the most and he isn't a shop assistant.

3 Jess works with animals and her work day is the earliest in the week.

4 The shop assistant works at the weekend.

5 The person who earns $20 an hour works on Fridays.

6 The dog walker[1] earns the least money.

7 Lola earns $2 more per hour than Sami.

Name	Job	$ per hour	Works on
Jess	*dog walker*		
Lola			
Sami			
Wei			

b) **Put these job features in order of how much you would want them for your future job (1 = most, 8 = least).**

– well-paid ☐
– working outside ☐
– the same hours every week ☐
– you don't need vocational training ☐
– working with animals ☐
– being the boss ☐
– working in a team ☐
– always being busy at work ☐

c) **Choose one job you might like to do in the future and one job you wouldn't like. Explain why, and use your answers in b) to help you.**

I might like to ______________________

I wouldn't like to ______________________

[1] **dog walker** *der/die Hundeausführer/in*

I can talk about jobs and future plans.

15 Lexi's first day at her new school

► SB, p. 88–90

Read sentences A–H and put them in the right order. Write numbers 1–8 in the boxes.

A That person was Kelsea, the sister of a popular junior. ☐
B Sharon came to help Lexi. ☐
C Lexi tried on an outfit for the first day at her new school. ☐
D Lexi decided to wear her normal clothes from now on. ☐
E In the cafeteria Lexi bumped into the person in front of her. ☐
F Lexi wanted advice from her friend Yuki. ☐
G She was cool and in the popular group, but she was mean to Lexi. ☐
H Sharon thought that Lexi was trying too hard with her clothes. ☐

16 Feelings in the story

► SB, p. 88–90

a) **Match the emojis to the feelings.**

1 worried ☐
2 stressed ☐
3 embarrassed ☐
4 excited ☐
5 surprised ☐
6 upset ☐

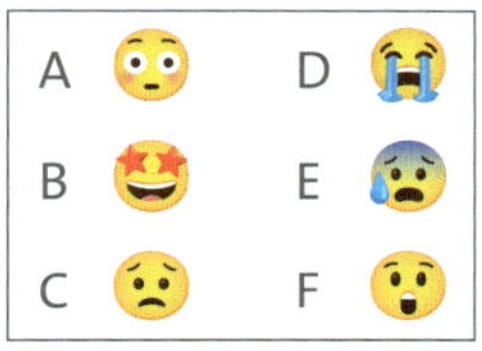

b) **Complete the table. Use the words in a) to help you.**

Lexi felt	(1) ________	when she didn't know what to wear for school.
	(2) ________	when she got lost several times.
	(3) ________	when she recognized Kelsea.
	(4) ________	when Kelsea talked about her clothes.
	(5) ________	when Kelsea kept going about Lexi.
	(6) ________	when when Sharon said they could eat together.

c) **Now answer the questions about the story.**

1 How was Kelsea mean?

She ________________________________

2 How was Sharon kind?

She ________________________________

17 Clothes

Look at the pictures and read sentences 1 and 2. Then write the missing words in the puzzle.

1 Carla is wearing a colourful ... (6), white ... (8) and red ... (4).

2 Mitch is wearing a white cycling ... (2), a blue ... (7), a yellow ... (1), brown ... (3) and black ... (5).

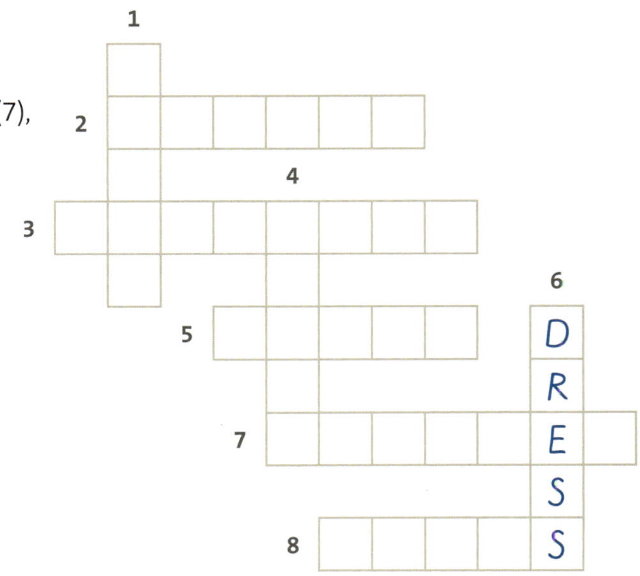

18 American English (AE) and British English (BE)

Write the English version of the words in the box in the right list.

candy • center • color • cookie • favorite • restroom • store • theater

-er in AE ↔ -re in BE	-or in AE ↔ -our in BE	different word	
______	______	s ______	t ______
______	______	b ______	s ______

19 A photo quiz in your students' book

Look at the photos in your book and write the missing words.

1 This is red, white and blue and has one star. It's the Texan ______________. *(page 76)*

2 Houston is the location of the Texan Space ______________. *(page 76)*

3 A Texan farm with animals is a ______________. *(page 77)*

4 Town centres are called ______________. *(page 77)*

5 In some towns like Fredericksburg a few people still speak Texan ______________. *(page 78)*

6 It's big, yellow and brings Texan kids to school. It's the school ______________. *(page 82)*

7 *Fifteen* is a ______________ by Taylor Swift. *(page 83)*

8 The animals that live in these stables are ______________. *(page 87)*

☒ 20 Opposites

a) **Write the opposites of these adjectives.**

1 interesting ↔ ___ ___ [___] ___ ___ ___

2 loud ↔ ___ ___ ___ [___] ___

3 mean ↔ ___ [___] ___ ___

4 safe ↔ ___ ___ ___ ___ ___ ___ ___ ___ [___]

5 expensive ↔ ___ ___ ___ ___ [___]

6 swift ↔ ___ ___ [___] ___

7 same ↔ ___ ___ ___ ___ ___ ___ ___ [___] ___

8 better ↔ ___ ___ ___ [___] ___

9 correct ↔ ___ ___ [___] ___ ___

10 private ↔ ___ ___ [___] ___ ___ ___

11 positive ↔ ___ [___] ___ ___ ___ ___ ___ ___

b) **The letters in blue make a word. Write the word in the sentence below.**

Babysitters are ____________________ for the children they are looking after.

21 SPEAKING Speak English well – American and British pronunciation differences

09

Three letters that are often pronounced differently in British and American English are *a*, *o* and *t*. Listen to the British and American versions of these sentences. Highlight the words or letters that sound different.

1 Can I take my water bottle to class?

2 I passed my driving test and bought a fast car.

3 The top student can't go to prom and that's totally unfair.

4 Where should you live? – Answers

► WB, p. 44

Count how many As, Bs and Cs you got in the quiz. Then check your results below.

- **Mostly As:** You should live in the city! You love having lots of people and activities around you and you don't like to be bored. You would be happiest in London or New York.
- **Mostly Bs:** You should live in a small town. The city is too loud for you, but the countryside is too quiet, so a small town is the perfect place for you.
- **Mostly Cs:** You want to be around nature and not people, so you should live in the country. A quiet house with your nearest neighbors miles away and nothing, but the sound of birds singing: that's the perfect home for you!

In Unit 3, the most interesting thing I learned was that ______________________

____

Write at least three new words you have learned for each of the topics in this unit.

Texas	Small-town life
______	______
School	**Jobs and future plans**
______	______

Imagine someone is interviewing you about what you learned in Unit 3.

Answer the questions with full sentences.

What surprised you most about American school life and why?

I was surprised to learn that ______________________

____

Which topic did you enjoy most in Unit 3 and why?

I enjoyed ______________________

____

Why would or wouldn't you like to visit Texas?

I'd like to visit Texas because ______________________

I'd wouldn't like to visit Texas because ______________________

What do you enjoy most in our English lessons?

I enjoy ______________________

What do you find hardest in our English lessons?

I find __________ *hardest.*

Remember:
Your best lesson is your last mistake!

What would you learn about in our English lessons if you could choose?

If I could choose, I would learn about ______________________

1 My project on the Space Center, Houston

Look online and find the missing information. Then write it below.

1 The price for adults (12+): ______

2 Hours the Space Center is open: ______

3 What can you do in the Food Lab? ______

4 What can you see on the NASA tram tour? ______

______

5 What can you see in the Starship Gallery? ______

6 What can you do in Independence Plaza? ______

______

7 Is there a security check when you go in? ______

► Check

2 My yearbook page

Complete your yearbook page with a picture. Then write messages on other students' yearbook pages. Don't forget to include the information in the box. For ideas look at exercise 11c) on page 48 in your workbook.

- class name
- message
- name
- photo

______

______

______

Erklär-film

1 Talking about work: My job interview

Write the correct verb forms for conditional sentences type 1.

1 I have an interview today. If I *get up* (get up) early, I ________ (find) the day less stressful.

2 I ________ (not feel) good at the interview if I ________ (not have) a good breakfast.

3 ________ (still have) time before the interview if my train ________ (arrive) late.

4 If they *give* (give) me the job, I ________ (celebrate) with my friends in the evening.

Tip: Find the *if*-part of the sentence and write this verb in the simple present. Then write the other verb in the will-future *(will / won't)*.

Remember

Mit Bedingungssätzen vom Typ 1 sagst du, was unter bestimmten Bedingungen passieren wird:
If you **get** a good job, you**'ll feel** happier.
if + **simple present** + **will/won't** + **verb**
Es ist durchaus wahrscheinlich, dass die Bedingungen erfüllt werden.

Erklär-film

2 Alicja's problem

Circle the correct words for conditional sentences type 2.

I find it hard to think about the future. If I knew / would know what I wanted to do, it wasn't / wouldn't be so stressful! My mum runs a business, but I know I wasn't / wouldn't be happy if I worked / would work for her. So what should I do? I guess I learned / would learn lots of useful things if I went / would go to college.
But I had / would have more money now if I got / would get a job. Of course, if I did / would do volunteer work, I helped / would help a lot of people. If it wasn't / wouldn't be so expensive, I went / would go travelling. Maybe I should work in another country. My English was / would be even better if I came / would come back to live in Texas after I leave school!

Tip: Find the *if*-part of the sentence and write this verb in the simple past tense. The other verb is with *would / wouldn't*.

Remember

Mit Bedingungssätzen vom Typ 2 sagst du, was unter bestimmten Bedingungen geschehen würde:
If you **got** a good job, you **would feel** happier.
if + **past tense** + **would/wouldn't** + **verb**
Es ist aber ziemlich unwahrscheinlich, dass die Bedingungen erfüllt werden.

▶ Check

3 New words in Unit 3

a) Complete the crossword.

1 *(across)* city centre *(American English)*

1 *(down) (verb)* suddenly not be there any more

2 when two or more countries fight

3 when someone always does what they say

4 how you feel when you are sad or hurt

5 this makes life stressful

6 quick

7 *(verb)* Don't stop, but … going!

8 *(verb)* want and hope for

9 when a killer uses a gun, e.g. in a school

10 the money that you earn

11 end of a letter: … faithfully

12 the teaching and learning that happen at school

13 to move from place to place: people get … here by car

14 rule for everyone in a country

15 *(verb)* opposite of 'lose'

16 I'm … if I have the care of another person.

17 *(verb)* move your head, meaning 'yes'

18 *(verb)* know about something, but not do anything about it

19 *(verb)* be responsible for an organisation

20 *(verb)* take and keep in your hand

21 catching animals from a river or the sea

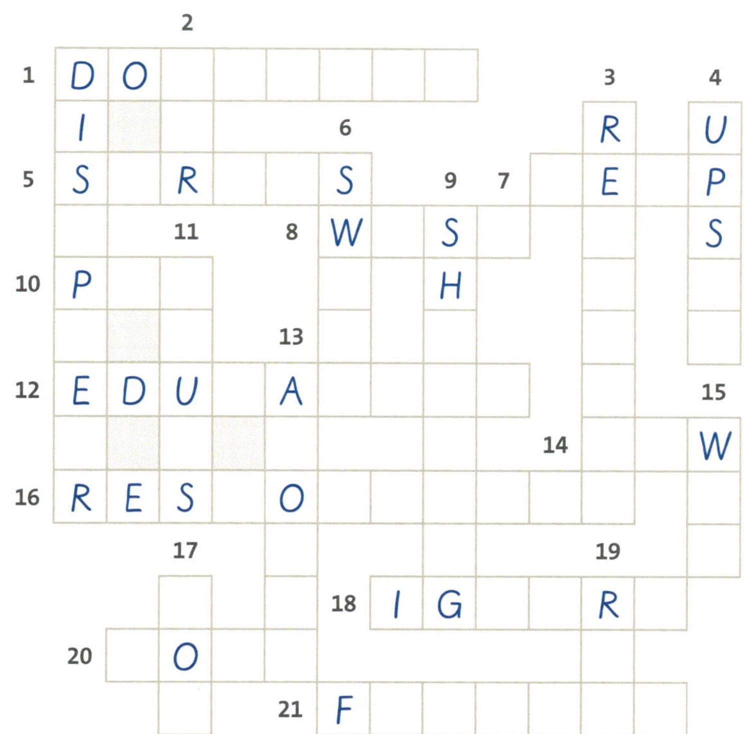

b) Write the full words.

1 vocab – vocabulary

2 exam – ______

3 sci-fi – ______

4 veg – ______

5 veggie – ______

6 intro – ______

► Check

Unit 4
California: State of contrasts

1 Words Describing California

► SB, p. 108

a) Circle eight adjectives in the wordsearch.

b) Highlight the letters you haven't used. They'll spell out a city in California.

____

S	A	F	N	B	O	R	I	N	G
	F	L		R	H	O	T	B	A
P	E	A	C	E	F	U	L	U	
N	C	T	I		S	N		S	C
M	O	D	E	R	N	D	R	Y	O

2 Speaking A Californian trip

► SB, p. 109

a) Partner B: Go to page 81.
Partner A: You are planning a trip to California. Your partner has found a website with a trip to Sequoia National Park. Ask your partner about it and write the main details.

1 How long is the trip? ________________
2 How do you travel? *By* ________________
3 Where do you sleep? *In* ________________
4 What does the trip cost? *$* ________________
5 What can you do there? *You can* ________________

____

b) Read the website about the Alcatraz Night Tour. Then answer your partner's questions about the trip.

ALCATRAZ NIGHT TOUR

A must-see for all history fans, but not if you're easily scared! Our night tours to this famous island include the return ferry trip and a guided tour around the museum – and you'll also experience the empty buildings in the dark. Are those strange noises just the wind or are they something scarier?! You can sleep one night on the island and look for ghosts! $120 per person. Must book online.

c) Discuss with your partner. Which trip would you prefer to do and why?

I think the trip to ... would be better because it's more exciting / cheaper / I'm interested in ...
Yes, I'd like to do that one too. / No, I'd prefer the trip to ... because I don't want to ... / I prefer ...

I can talk about California.

3 Reading **Eureka**

► SB, p. 110

a) **Read the travel guide to Riley's town of Eureka and tick (✓) the three correct sentences.**

b) **Now write the line(s) in the text where you found the answer for each sentence.**

	a)	b)
1 Eureka is by the sea.	☐	☐
2 The town has always been called Eureka.	☐	☐
3 Eureka has lots of natural areas.	☐	☐
4 Eureka looks very different and modern today.	☐	☐
5 The town is only interesting for people who like history.	☐	☐
6 There are lots of places to go shopping in Eureka.	☐	☐

A traditional building in Eureka

History is everywhere in this beautiful town on the Californian coast – even the name 'Eureka' comes from an old Greek[1] word that means, 'I have found it'. This is because in the 1850s, lots of people came to the area to dig for gold. However, it's also important to remember that Native Americans lived here for thousands of years before that, and they called it Jaroujiji, which means 'where you sit and rest'. And with all our beautiful beaches and forests to enjoy, that's also a perfect name!

Eureka is famous for its traditional colorful buildings – lots of the town looks almost as it did in the past. Walk through the town, visit all the main sights and museums, and you'll feel like you have traveled back in time!

But don't worry, Eureka isn't only about the past. The town offers lots of other activities too, such as skateboarding, outdoor sports and a zoo, as well as hundreds of interesting little stores and a night market. There's something here for everyone, so you won't be bored!

Erklär-film

4 Language **Riley's game**

► SB, p. 110

Riley is showing a game on her phone to her dad, who doesn't know much about games. Write the missing words (*am*, *is*, *are* or *isn't* or *aren't*) to help her explain it.

This is my character, and I have to run around and find all the magic blue boxes. Look, my score (1) ________ shown up there. But if I collect a red box, the points (2) ________ added to my score – they (3) ________ taken away! And there are monsters too, so if I (4) ________ seen by them, I'll be chased. I have to be really careful because the game (5) ________ saved automatically[2], so if my character (6) ________ killed before I save it, I'll lose all my points!

[1] **Greek** *griechisch* [2] **automatically** *automatisch*

5 LANGUAGE Making a game character

► SB, p. 111

Complete the notes about how video game characters are made. Write the past participle of the verbs in brackets to form the passive.

Ideas are collected (collect).

↓

The best ideas are ________ (chose).

↓

The character is ________ (draw) by an artist.

→

The character's actions are ________ (code) by a programmer.

↑

The character's voice is ________ (record).

↑

The first demo is ________ (test).

→

Different opinions are ________ (give).

↓

Any problems are ________ (fix).

↓

The character is ________ (add) to the game.

6 LANGUAGE Riley's dream robot

► SB, p. 111

Riley's dream AI robot can do lots of things for her.

a) Write the past participles of the four verbs.

b) Complete the sentences in the passive. Choose *is* or *are* in each sentence.

a) brush: brushed

b) Riley's teeth are brushed.

a) do: done

b) Riley's homework is ________.

a) cook: ________

b) Riley's meals ________.

a) tidy: ________

b) Riley's desk ________.

a) make: ________

b) Riley's bed ________.

a) clean: ________

b) Riley's shoes ________.

7 Listening Can robots write music?

▶ SB, p. 113

10 a) Listen to part one of the podcast. Are Aaliyah and Grayson positive (P) or negative (N) about AI?

Aaliyah: ______ Grayson: ______

11 b) Think about the pieces of music you've just heard. Tick (✓) the piece that you think is written by AI. Then listen to part 2 of the podcast and check your answer.

Piece 1: ☐ Piece 2: ☐

10–11 c) Read these opinion phrases. Then listen to both parts of the podcast again and write the order Aaliyah and Grayson use these phrases.

- ☐ Don't you think that …?
- ☐ You have a point that …
- ☐ Can't you see that …?
- ☐ I hear what you're saying, but …
- ☐ I don't agree with you.

d) Who thinks this: Aaliyah (A), Grayson (G) or both (A&G)?

1 AI can do anything creative. ☐
2 You can't write good music without feelings. ☐
3 AI music can be better than music written by real people. ☐
4 The AI piece is not as difficult. ☐
5 Musicians should be paid for their work. ☐
6 Robots should do the boring jobs. ☐

8 Writing Is using AI OK?

▶ SB, p. 113

Alice, a student, asks AI to check her English homework and correct any mistakes. Is that OK? Why? Or why not? Write about 40 words to give your opinion.

I think it's OK because …
- Alice has done the work.
- AI can help her to see / find mistakes.
- she can learn more if she checks her work herself with AI.
- she can get her answers faster.
- can add her own ideas.

I think it isn't OK because …
- Alice will learn more if she does it herself.
- it isn't fair / it's cheating.
- she may become lazy.
- the teacher can't know if Alice has really understood.

I think / I don't think this is OK because ______________________

____

____

____

I can have a discussion about AI.

9 A Native American timeline[1]

► SB, p. 114

a) Read Tiana's essay on page 114 of your book again and put the events (A–F) in the right order.

A European people arrived in America. ☐

B Many Native children died in government boarding schools. ☐

C Native Americans lived in America. 1

D Native children were taken away from their parents by the government. ☐

E The government gave back the Yurok some of their land. ☐

F White people killed Native Americans. ☐

b) Put the events (A–F) in the right order in the timeline.

○ ○ ○ ○ ○ ○ →

10 LISTENING Going to a powwow

► SB, p. 115

a) Look at the picture and write notes to answer the questions.

1 What can you see in the photo?

____

____

2 What do you remember about powwows?

____

____

At a powwow

12

b) Listen to Tiana's dad Cree talking to their neighbour Donna. Then complete the sentences.

1 Donna wants to ______________________________

2 She doesn't want to ______________________________

12

c) Listen again and decide if each sentence is true (T) or false (F).

1 The powwow is next month. ☐

2 Only Native Americans can go to powwows. ☐

3 Only one tribe goes to each powwow. ☐

4 Drums are an important part of the powwow. ☐

5 You should always walk around the circle, not through it. ☐

6 Visitors should wear traditional Native American clothes at a powwow. ☐

7 Photos are not allowed at powwows. ☐

[1] **timeline** *Zeitleiste*

11 LANGUAGE Native American inventions[1]

▸ SB, p. 115

Many things we use today were invented by Native Americans. Circle the correct answers: *was / wasn't / were / weren't*

1 Did you know that the sport lacrosse was / wasn't invented[2] by Native Americans in what is now New York? It was / wasn't played by over 100 players at a time!

2 Today, kayaking is a popular sport around the world, but kayaks were / weren't used by Native Americans to travel and find food 4,000 years ago! The first kayaks were / weren't made of wood[3] or plastic as now, but animal skins.

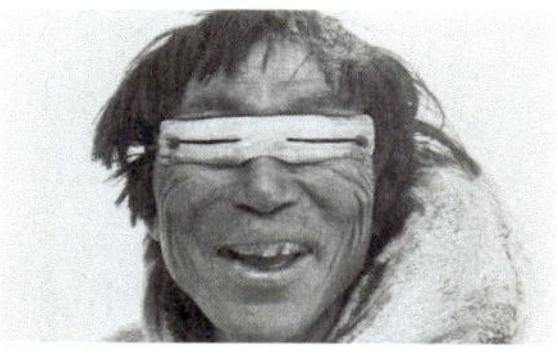

3 Famous people often wear sunglasses to look cool, but they were / weren't invented in Hollywood! Native Americans in Alaska and Canada made special glasses out of wood or parts of animals, and small holes were / weren't cut into them so that their eyes were / weren't hurt by the sun on the snow.

4 We eat corn in different ways today, from popcorn to cornflakes, but corn was / wasn't discovered by Europeans. It was / wasn't first grown by Native Americans 10,000 years ago and then Europeans was / were taught how to grow and cook with it much later.

☒ 12 LANGUAGE The Chimariko people

▸ SB, p. 115

Complete the sentences. Use the passive in the simple past. Remember that you must write two words: *was* or *were* + *past participle of the verb*.

The Chimariko were a Native American tribe in north-western California until the 1930s. Their land (1) *was* *taken* (take) by white people who were looking for gold in the 1850s. The rivers (2) ________ ________ (make) dirty by the gold workers, so lots of the fish (the Chimariko's main food) (3) ________ ________ (kill). Traditional Chimariko houses (4) ________ ________ (make) of wood and men and women lived separately.

shells

Shells[4] (5) ________ ________ (use) by the Chimariko people for money, but they weren't (6) ________ (keep) in a money bag – they (7) ________ ________ (wear) around the neck. Another tradition was that every man (8) ________ ________ (give) a feather[5] to wear when he won a fight.

[1] **invention** *Erfindung* [2] (to) **invent** *erfinden* [3] **wood** *das Holz* [4] **shell** *die Muschel* [5] **feather** *die Feder*

13 MEDIATION A Native American influencer

► Digital help ► SB, p. 117

A new kind of social media star

Naiomi Glasses

Naiomi Glasses is a different kind of influencer: not the cool, rich person wearing the latest fashion, but a skateboarding Native American who uses social media to teach people about her culture. More and more teens are sharing her videos on social media.

Glasses, who is from the Diné tribe, was taught to skateboard at the age of five by her brother. At first, she got followers because of her amazing tricks, but then she started to talk more about Native American culture. In a recent video, she showed some traditional Diné handbags, which weren't made of leather or plastic but of wool from her own sheep.

As well as teaching her followers about Native American crafts and fashion, Glasses has a strong message about kindness. She was born with a cleft lip[1], which meant her face looked different, and she was bullied at school because of it. But even though she wasn't treated kindly by other students, she stayed strong and believed in herself. And she's here to tell other young people to do the same.

a) Read the web article and write the German for these words and phrases:

1 the latest fashion *(line 2)* ____________ 2 handbags *(line 9)* ____________

3 leather *(line 9)* ____________ 4 crafts *(line 11)* ____________

b) Complete the notes in German about the article.

1 Naiomi Glasses ist eine ungewöhnliche Influencerin, weil sie ____________

____

____________.

2 Zunächst waren ihre Videos beliebt wegen ____________.

3 Sie fertigt u. a. ____________.

4 In der Schule ____________.

5 Ihre Botschaft an junge Menschen ist, ____________

____________.

c) Find five examples of the passive in the simple past in the article and highlight them.

[1] **cleft lip** *die Hasenscharte*

I can talk about Native American history.

14 LANGUAGE Camping tips

▸ Digital help ▸ SB, p. 119

Complete the camping tips with the words from the box. You have to use some of them more than once.

although • because • so that (2x) • unless (2x)

Camping tips

- ✓ Check the weather (1) ______________ you can pack the right clothes for rain or sun.
- ✓ (2) ______________ open fires are OK, remember to bring a camping cooker.
- ✓ Bring a first aid kit[1], (3) ______________ it's better to call 911 if someone is badly hurt.
- ✓ Never feed wild animals (4) ______________ it could make them ill.
- ✓ Bring a camp bed (5) ______________ you like sleeping on the cold, hard ground!
- ✓ Sleep with your clothes next to you (6) ______________ they are warm in the morning.

15 WRITING A camping cartoon

▸ SB, p. 119

Look at the cartoon and write at least five sentences about it. You should include:

- the people, places and actions
- why the cartoon is funny
- your opinion about the cartoon

bear • boy • campsite • chair • fire • trees

In the cartoon, I can see / there is / there are ...
In the foreground / background, ...
He is / It is / They are ...
The cartoon is funny because he thinks..., but really ...
I think the cartoon is...

____

____

____

____

____

____

____

[1] **first aid kit** *das Erste-Hilfe-Set*

16 Listening A scary camping experience

▸ SB, p. 119

13 a) Which animal did Eric meet on his camping trip? ______________________

13 b) Listen to the radio interview and circle the correct answers.

1 Eric went camping alone / with friends.

2 He met a mountain lion which wanted to eat his food / him.

3 The animal hurt Eric / didn't move.

4 Eric shouted and waved his arms / talked quietly and walked slowly backwards[1].

5 Then Eric ran away / climbed to higher ground.

6 The animal followed him / ate his food.

a mountain lion

13 c) Read the sentences below, then listen again: Which advice is right for which animal? Tick (✓).

	mountain lions	bears	both
1 Don't camp alone.	☐	☐	☐
2 Don't leave out food.	☐	☐	☐
3 Shout and wave your arms up and down.	☐	☐	☐
4 Stay still or move slowly backwards.	☐	☐	☐
5 Talk calmly to the animal.	☐	☐	☐
6 Try to look bigger.	☐	☐	☐
7 Climb to higher ground.	☐	☐	☐
8 Throw something at it.	☐	☐	☐
9 Use pepper spray.	☐	☐	☐

d) Write at least five sentences about what you should and shouldn't do when camping in a national park. Use the advice in c) to help you.

You must ______________________

You mustn't ______________________

If you __________ *you should* __________

____

You shouldn't ______________________

[1] **backwards** *rückwärts*

I can talk about nature in California.

17 Tell the story of the film

► SB, p. 123

a) **Complete the text with words from the box. You won't need all the words.**

angry • animals • buy • changed • connected • goat • land • legend • life • saved • sold • water

Some men decided they could put (1) ______________ from the river in bottles and sell it. But when the river was dry, the (2) ______________ and people disappeared from the area. The water company wanted to (3) ______________ the water on the (4) ______________ that was owned by Angie's grandfather. Angie was (5) ______________ with him when he (6) ______________ it to them. But then Angie's grandfather (7) ______________ his mind and (8) ______________ his water to the river. This helped so many other people that Angie's grandfather became a (9) ______________.

b) **Watch the video again and check your answers.**

18 The film in pictures

► SB, p. 123

Look at the photos and write the events from the film that they show.

A

Angie goes ______________

____

B

Angie and her grandfather ______________

____

C

Angie's grandfather ______________

when he ______________

D

Angie's grandfather ______________

____

19 Prepositions

Complete the sentences with the correct prepositions from the box.

about • by • of • out • to • up

1 You can add AI technology __________ your devices.

2 What are the pros and cons __________ AI?

3 I have to write a text __________ AI.

4 I love waking __________ early when I go camping.

5 Our path was blocked __________ a tree.

6 The fire was so big we couldn't put it __________.

20 Wildlife words

Write the names of these animals.

1

____

2

____

3

____

4

____

5

____

6

____

21 Verbs in Unit 4

Write the right verbs from the box. You don't need all the verbs.

ban • burn • change • cheat • force • predict • survive • taste • tie

1 Mmm! These s'mores ______________ good!

2 Sometimes I want to go camping, but then I ______________ my mind.

3 I know I shouldn't ______________ when I have an exam.

4 I think we should ______________ sexism and racism.

5 Can AI really ______________ what I want to say?

6 You can't ______________ children to be good. You have to give them a good example.

22 Writing Describe a picture

Look at the photo. Describe what you can see. Say what people here mustn't do and say why you would or wouldn't like to be here. Use words in the box or your own words.

bears • camp • nature • rubbish • tall • tent • tree

I can see ______________________________

If you camp here you mustn't ______________ *because* ______________

____

I would / wouldn't like ______________ *because* ______________

23 Speaking Speak English well: the letter G

a) Sort these words into the two 'g' sounds in the table below. One word doesn't fit.

dangerous • dig • game • giant • green • grow • gun • intelligence • large • sign

G like [g] in 'go'	G like [ʤ] in 'Germany'

b) Which word doesn't fit and why? ______________ *because* ______________

14 c) Listen and check your answers.

How I found the topics in Unit 4:

boring • difficult • easy • exciting • interesting • sad • scary • shocking

Places in California: ____________________

AI and technology: ____________________

Native Americans: ____________________

Nature: ____________________

Even the best fall over sometimes, but they always get up again.

I know ...

– some famous places in California: ____________________

____

– some technology words: ____________________

– some words about Native American culture: ____________________

____

– some Californian wildlife: ____________________

I can ...

– use the passive in the simple present tense:

English ... (speak) all over the world. → ____________________

– use the passive in the simple past tense:

Our school ... (build) many years ago. → ____________________

My progress[1]

Look back at your learner log from Unit 2 on page 37.
What can you do now that was difficult before?

I got better at ... • I find it easier to ... • I can ... much better. • I'm better at ...

____

____

____

[1] **progress** *der Fortschritt*

1 State abbreviations

a) Every US state has a code. For example, CA is the state code for California. Look at the six codes and guess the six states. You can do research online to help you.

1 TX ______ 2 FL ______ 3 LA ______

4 AK ______ 5 NJ ______ 6 OK ______

b) Write the codes for the two states. The two codes make one word.

1 Georgia, Maine GA + ME = game

2 Wisconsin, North Dakota ___ + ___ = ______

3 Colorado, Delaware ___ + ___ = ______

4 Massachusetts, New York ___ + ___ = ______

▶ Check

2 AI mistakes

Riley asked AI to make a picture of a 'baby carrot'. This is what it made. Explain what AI did wrong.

▶ Check

3 My game character

Design your own video game character. Draw them and make notes about their personality and skills. Use the words from the box or your own ideas.

able to • female • fight • fly • help • injustice • male • reliable • strong • talk ...

1 Using new technology

Erklär-film

Complete the sentences.
Use the passive in the simple present.

~~clean~~ • cook • do • empty • make • take • wash

Remember

Im **simple present** bildest du das Passiv mit **am/is/are** und dem **past participle**:
*Music **is** sometimes **written** by AI.*

I think AI is amazing.

Our house (1) is cleaned *by a robot.*

Our shopping (2) ____________ by a robot.

Our rubbish (3) ____________ out by a robot.

Our car (4) ____________ by a robot.

The dishwasher (5) ____________ .

The beds (6) ____________ .

And our meals (7) ____________ by a robot.

Nice joke, Sam – but I don't believe you.

2 A terrible trip

Erklär-film

Complete the diary[1].
Write the verbs in the simple past passive.

Remember

Im **simple past** bildest du das Passiv mit **was/were** und dem **past participle**:
*All my things **were stolen**. Nothing **was left**.*

Dear diary,

That's it – I am NEVER going camping again!

I spent the weekend with my cousins in the Redwood National Park.

I (1) was told (tell) that it would be sunny, but it rained the whole time! It was so boring because my charger (2) ____________ (leave) at home, so my phone (3) ____________ (not charge) all weekend and I couldn't use it. We (4) ____________ (wake) every morning by the sounds of animals and all my snacks (5) ____________ (eat) by little insects, which was really annoying. And then I fell over while we were hiking, but I was lucky and my leg (6) ____________ (not break) by the fall, but my clothes (7) ____________ (make) really dirty! Camping isn't for me!

▶ Check

[1] **diary** *das Tagebuch*

3 Explaining a chart

Complete the sentences about the information form the chart.
Use words in the box. If you need help, look at page 124 in your book.

die • fewer • kill • go up • go down

The number of people who are killed on California's roads

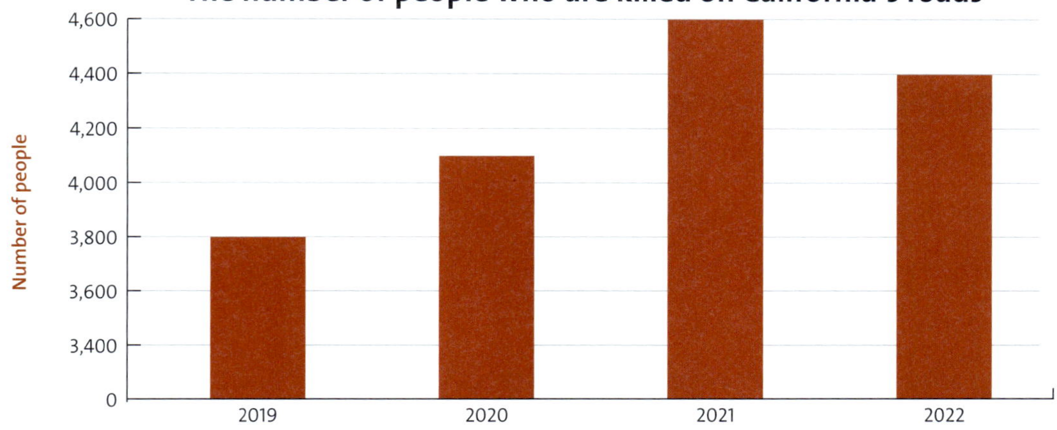

Data Source: https://www.mesrianilaw.com/blog/california-car-accident-statistics/

1 In 2019 3,800 people ____________________ on California's roads.

2 This number ____________________ between 2019 and 2021,

but ____________________ in 2022.

3 ____________________ on the roads in 2022.

4 The chart shows that the number of people who die on Californian roads ____________________.

4 New words in Unit 4

Find four words for each group and write them in the table.
The words are all in the unit.

AI • ~~bear~~ • burn • data • deer • firefighter • image • ocean • put out • river • salmon • smoke • special effects • tap • turn off • wolf

wildlife	tech words	water	fire
bear			

▸ Check

Unit 5
Canada: The northern neighbour

1 What do you know about Canada?

► SB, p. 141

Read the sentences. Are they true (T) or false (F)?

1 The Canadian flag is red and white, with a red maple leaf on it. ☐
2 Canada is larger in size than the USA. ☐
3 The leader of the country is the president. ☐
4 The name 'Canada' comes from a French word that means 'village'. ☐
5 A moose is a big Canadian mouse. ☐
6 Vancouver and the Niagara Falls are on different sides of Canada. ☐
7 Canada has lots of islands. ☐
8 Lacrosse is an indoor sport, a bit like table tennis. ☐

2 READING Canadian pancakes

► SB, p. 141

a) **Read the recipe for Canadian pancakes.**
Warning: The sentences are in the wrong order! Write the numbers 1-5 in the right order.

Canadian pancakes

a bowl

You need:

120 g flour
240 ml milk
3 eggs
maple syrup[1]

1. Separate the white and yellow parts of the eggs. Add the yellow parts to the mixture in the bowl.
2. Mix the flour and milk in a bowl.
3. Eat the pancakes hot with maple syrup.
4. Put some of the mixture into a hot frying pan. Cook the pancake for a few minutes on each side until some of it is brown.
5. Mix the white parts of the eggs quickly until they are thick, then add them to the mixture.

The right order of the sentences in the recipe is:

2 ☐ ☐ ☐ ☐

b) **What else could you put on the pancakes? Write at least three things.**

____
____
____
____
____

[1] **maple syrup** *der Ahornsirup*

I can talk about Canada. ✓

3 Fun facts about Canada

► SB, p. 143

a) Do you know or can you guess the right answers? Tick (✓) A, B or C.

1 Canada's coldest recorded temperature in Snag, Yukon, in 1947, was ...

A - 63.0°C ☐ B - 45.0°C ☐
C - 37.0°C ☐

2 Superman was created by Canadians ...

A in 1978. ☐ B in 1933. ☐
C in 1956. ☐

3 Canada has the world's largest natural ice rink. It's ...

A 20.5 kilometres long. ☐
B 7.8 kilometres long. ☐
C 4.7 kilometres long. ☐

Rideau Canal Skateway

4 Canada has ...

A the longest coast in the world. ☐
B the second longest coast in the world after Russia. ☐
C the third longest coast in the world after Russia and Australia. ☐

5 In some areas of Canada drivers do not lock[1] their cars because they want to make sure that people can escape from ...

A bears. ☐ B the police. ☐
C beavers. ☐

A beaver

6 The name Canada comes from ...

A the noise of a train on a wood railway. ☐
B a First Nation (Laurentian) word that means 'village'. ☐
C the song of a small North American bird. ☐

b) Find out!

1 Canada held the Olympic Games three times. Find out if they were Winter or Summer Games, where they took place and when.

____

____

____

2 Is it true that there is a prison for polar bears[2] in Canada? If so, find out where it is. When was it started? Why?

____

____

[1] (to) **lock** *abschließen* [2] **polar bear** *der Eisbär*

4 Reading Gold

In August 1896 gold was found in the Klondike region of northwest Canada. In the next two years, 100,000 people left San Francisco and Seattle to try and find gold in the Klondike. It was difficult to get there, so only 40,000 people arrived. 4,000 people found gold, but mostly so little that they did not become rich. Here is the story of Jim, one of the men who went to Klondike.
Read the story and answer the questions in the reading log.

July 17, 1897

Gold! Everybody in my streetcar[1] here in Seattle is talking about gold. That's because a ship called 'Portland' came into the harbour today with large pieces of gold from a region they call Klondike, in northwest Canada. And people say there's a lot more gold there.

My reading log

1 How did Jim hear about the gold in Klondike?

July 19, 1897

I had a drink with Sam and Jody today. Like me, they are streetcar drivers here in Seattle. And all we talked about was the gold in Klondike. Looking for gold sounds more exciting than driving a streetcar on the same route every day!

"If I find gold in Klondike," I said to Jenny later, "I'll buy you the most beautiful dress in the world!"

Skagway, Alaska

July 28, 1897

We're on our way to Klondike! I'm not really sure where Klondike is, but Sam, Jody and I are going there. We're on the 'Queen', a boat that will take us to Skagway in Alaska. From there, people say, we have to walk to Klondike. I hope it's not too far!

October 15, 1897

We're still in Skagway and we're in trouble. We have to bring food for one year to Klondike because there are no towns or villages there. That's 520 kilos! So we need a horse to carry our stuff. But now there are thousands of people here on their way to Klondike, and they all need horses. So, horses are now really expensive and we'll have to work here to earn the money for a horse.

March 16, 1898

We left Skagway two days ago with our horse 'Vulcan', and we're on our way over the mountains to Klondike. It's a small path, but it's full of people on their way to Klondike. We spent the night in our tent and we froze. People say it was minus fifty degrees Celsius here in January. I dreamt of Jenny in an amazing new dress.

My reading log

2 Who do you think Jenny is?
3 Can you understand Jim? Or do you think he is stupid? Explain your opinion.
4 What do you think will happen next?

[1] **streetcar** (AmE) *die Straßenbahn*

March 21, 1898

Thank God we are down from the mountains. It was so cold up there and the path was so small that people and horses died every day. And one terrible day Jody fell from the path … We never saw him again. We are now next to a lake. I first thought this was Klondike because hundreds of men are working here. But they aren't looking for gold. They are cutting down trees and building boats because Klondike is still 800 kilometers away, down the Yukon River.
So, Sam and I need to build a boat too.
But we don't know how.

My reading log
5 Why are men building boats?

June 15, 1898

We built our boat together with some other men, and then we came down the river. It was strange: We were in wild, empty country, but the river was completely full of boats. People say more than seven thousand boats came down the river to Klondike last month! And now we are looking for gold. I thought we might find gold in the rivers here, but we have to dig tunnels deep into the ground. It's hard work.

My reading log
6 Look at the photo of gold diggers in 1898. What do you think life was like for them? Give examples like: *dangerous – because there were wild animals.*

September 9, 1898

Gold! Today we found gold! I was working with Sam and suddenly we saw a bit of yellow in the earth – just a small bit of gold, but enough to pay for our journey here. This evening Sam and I celebrated in a saloon bar in Dawson City (Yes, a city: the population was 500 eighteen months ago, it's now 30,000!).
And I'm so excited. Maybe we'll find more gold tomorrow?

December 12, 1898

That's it, we have decided to leave Klondike. There are thousands of people here and very few are finding gold. And the work is difficult because it's so cold. The ground is so hard that we have to make fires before we can dig into the earth. And we never found any more gold.

But Sam and I have decided to go to Nome, in Alaska, because people say gold has been found there. Maybe we'll be luckier this time?

I just hope that Jenny hasn't forgotten me. I have written to her, but I haven't got any replies. Maybe her letters have got lost in the post?

My reading log
7 What is your opinion of Jim at the end of the story? Has your opinion changed?

▸ WB, p. 83

I can understand a story about Canada.

5 Words about Canada

Complete the puzzle with words about Canada.

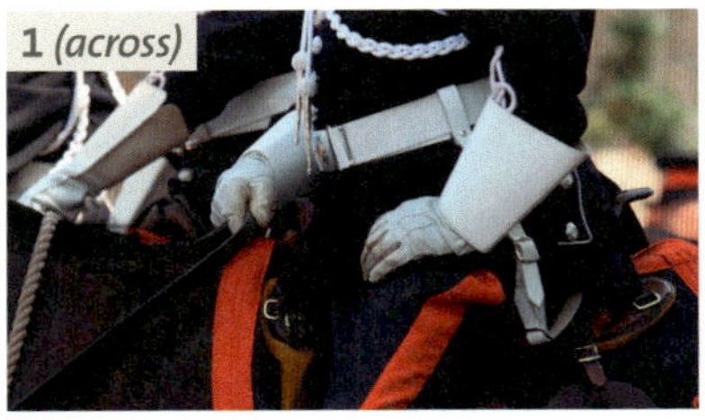
1 *(across)*

1 *(down) (two words)*

2 *(two words)*

3

4

5

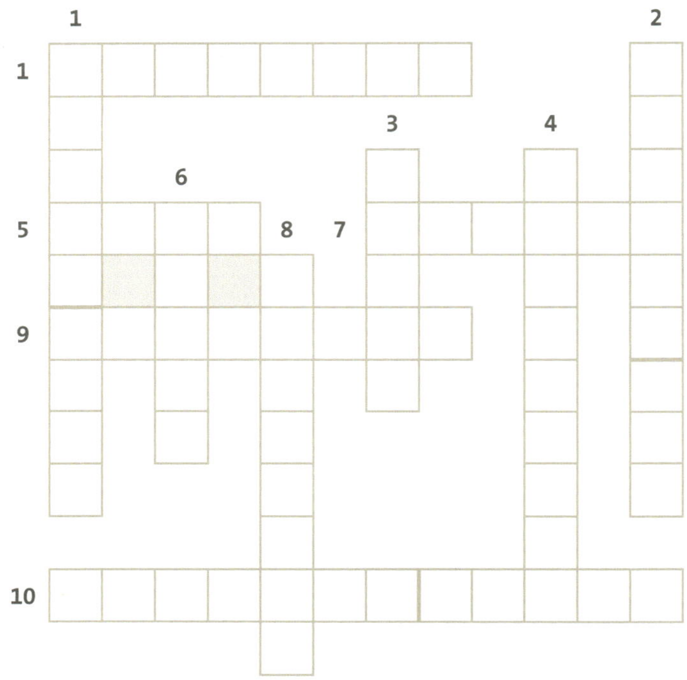

6

7 *(capital of Canada)*

8

9

10 *(two words)*

My favourite thing about Unit 5 was ____________________

____

My progress[1]

Complete the sentences to say how confident you are about the *I can* statements in this unit. You can use the ideas from the box or use your own ideas.

the easiest • easy • a bit difficult • the most difficult

It doesn't matter what others are doing, it matters what you are doing.

I can talk about Canada. This is ____________ for me because ____________

____

I can understand a longer story. This is ____________ for me because

____

Looking back at this year

Look at your learner logs from units 1 to 4. Write six sentences to explain ...

- which units you found easiest, most difficult, most interesting and why.
- which area of the USA or Canada you would most like to visit and why.
- any other parts of the USA or Canada you would like to learn about.
- how you'll want to get better in English in the next year.

1 I found ________ the easiest because ____________

2 I found ________ the most difficult because ____________

3 I found ________ the most interesting because ____________

4 I'd like to visit ____________

5 I'd like to learn about ____________

6 Next year, to get better in English, I'll ____________

____

____

____

[1] **progress** *der Fortschritt*

1 A special competition

a) There's a hair freezing competition at the Takhini Hot Springs in the Yukon in Canada every winter. Look at the pictures (A–D). Who would you choose as the winner and why?

I would choose picture ______ because I think it is ______

______

______

A

B

C

D

b) To freeze your hair, you have to put your head into hot water and then stand still in the cold air. If the air is -20 degrees Celsius or colder, your hair will freeze. Would you like to take part in the competition? Why or why not?

I would / wouldn't like to take part because ______

______

2 Canadian words

Try to find words and places linked to Canada for as many letters of the alphabet as possible. Some of them might not be possible, but you can do research to help you.

A – ______	I/J – ______	R – ______
B – ______	K – ______	S – ______
C – ______	L – ______	______
D – ______	M – ______	T – ______
E – ______	N – ______	U – ______
F – ______	O – ______	V – ______
G – ______	P – ______	W – ______
H – ______	Q – ______	X/Y/Z – ______

Unit 1 Topic 3 | Exercise 14

▶ WB, p. 18 ▶ SB, p. 27

a) Partner B: You are in another city. Look at the subway map. Listen to your partner and tell them the way. Use the colours of the subway lines.

Take the ... line to ...
Change at ... Then take the ...

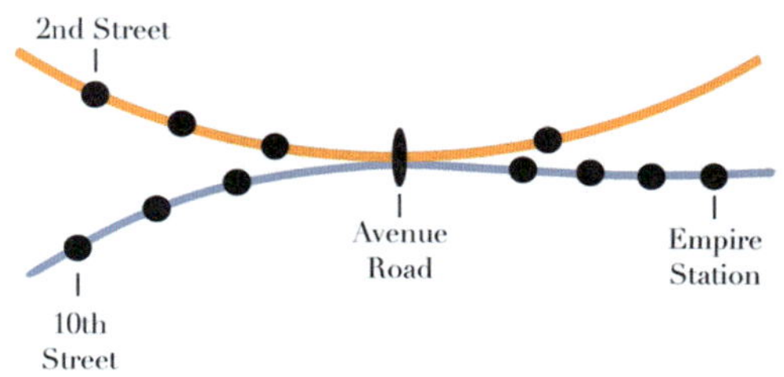

b) Now ask your partner for help. You are at Riverside Park and you want to get to Green Stadium. Ask you your partner for help and write the information.

Excuse me, can you help me, please?
I don't really understand the map.
How can I ... from ... to ...?

Take the ______________ line to ______________.

Change at ______________________________.

Then take the ______________________________ line.

Unit 4 Lead-in | Exercise 2

▶ WB, p. 58 ▶ SB, p. 109

a) Partner B: Read the text and then answer your partner's questions about the trip.

SEQUOIA NATIONAL PARK TRIP

Calling all nature lovers! You mustn't miss our private 2-day trip to Sequoia National Park. Our experienced guides will drive you deep into the park where we have comfortable tents already set up. Then they will take you on a hike through the forest to show you the amazing trees, plants and animals. You'll sleep well after a meal cooked on the campfire and a peaceful night looking at the stars. $250 per person.

b) Your partner has found a trip called Alcatraz Night Tour. Ask your partner about it and make notes about the trip.

1 How do you travel? By ______________

2 How long is the trip? ______________

3 Where do you sleep? On ______________.

4 What does the trip cost? $ ______________

5 What can you do there? You get a ______________.

You experience ______________.

You can look for ______________.

c) Discuss with your partner. Which trip would you prefer to do and why?

I think the trip to ... would be better because it's more exciting / cheaper / I'm interested in / ...
Yes, I'd like to do that one too. / No, I'd rather do the trip to ... because I don't want to... / I prefer...

Unit 2 Topic 3 | Exercise 10

► WB, p. 33 ► SB, p. 55

Partner B: You and your partner have different copies of the recipe. Take turns to
- ask a question and write the missing information in the recipe.
- listen to your partner and give the missing information.

Your partner asks the first question.

Note: Don't read everything – just give your partner the missing information.

How to make jambalaya

frying pan with lid

chicken stock

celery

garlic

cajun seasoning

1 *Answer your partner's question: You ...*

1 **You will need:**
- a frying pan with a lid
- chicken, sausage, chicken stock[1]
- celery, a green pepper, a tomato and an onion
- garlic, spices and cajun seasoning
- rice, some oil[2], flour, salt and pepper

2 *How long should I fry the chicken?*

2 Put some oil in a large frying pan. Fry the chicken ______________________________ ______________________________.

3 *Answer your partner's question: You ...*

3 When the chicken is brown, put it on a dish.

4 *What do I have to do with the sausage after frying it?*

4 Now fry both sides of the sausage, then ______________________________.

5 *Answer your partner's question: You ...*

5 Add some flour to the frying pan and mix well. Add the onion, garlic, celery, green peppers and fry for three minutes.

6 *How do I have to cut the tomato?*

6 Cut the tomato ______________________________. and put it in the frying pan with salt, pepper, spices and cajun seasoning. Mix well.

7 *Answer your partner's question: You ...*

7 Add the chicken stock and the rice. When the stock is really hot, add the chicken and sausage.

8 *How long should I cook the meat and vegetables?*

8 Put a lid on the frying pan and cook for ______________________________.

And that's it. Enjoy!

[1] **chicken stock** *die Geflügelbrühe* [2] **oil** *das Öl*

Unit 5 Story Reading log

▸ WB, pp. 76–77

Possible answers for the reading log

1 After a boat arrived with gold from Klondike, everybody talked about it a lot.

2 Jenny could be Jim's wife, or maybe she's his girlfriend.

3 I can understand Jim because he wants to earn money and he has a boring job. /
I think he is stupid if he leaves a good job and a wife or girlfriend to go on a dangerous trip to Klondike, although he doesn't know where it is.

4 I think Jim will find gold in Klondike / will die in Klondike / ...

5 Men are building boats because they have to go down the Yukon River to get to Klondike.

6 Uncomfortable –
because the men lived in tents and it was very cold in winter;
because there was little food, and they had to work very hard.

7 I could understand why Jim went to Klondike, but now I think he is stupid because he should come back to Jenny, and not go to Nome.

Typical tasks	Häufige Arbeitsanweisungen
Act out the conversation / scene.	Führt das Gespräch / die Szene vor.
Answer the questions / partner B's questions.	Beantworte die Fragen / Partner/in Bs Fragen.
Ask questions.	Stelle Fragen.
Check with your partner.	Überprüfe mit deiner Partnerin / deinem Partner.
Choose the correct verbs / a person / ...	Wähle die richtigen Verben / eine Person / ...
Circle the correct word / correct verb / ...	Kreise das richtige Wort / das richtige Verb / ... ein.
Compare the pictures / your answers / ... with a partner.	Vergleiche die Bilder / deine Antworten / ... mit einem/r Partner/in.
Complete the questions / table / ...	Vervollständige die Fragen / Tabelle / ...
Correct the false / wrong sentences / answers.	Berichtige die falschen Sätze / Antworten.
Cross out (~~cross out~~) the numbers / wrong things / ...	Streiche die Nummern / die falschen Dinge / ... durch.
Describe the picture.	Beschreibe das Bild.
Draw pictures / lines / ...	Zeichne / Male Bilder / Linien / ...
Explain why.	Begründe (deine Antwort).
Fill the gaps with the correct words.	Vervollständige die Lücken mit den richtigen Wörtern.
Find the answers / correct picture / ...	Finde die Antworten / das richtige Bild / ...
Give reasons.	Begründe (deine Antwort).
Highlight the letters / words / ...	Markiere die Buchstaben / Wörter / ...
Listen again.	Höre nochmal zu.
Listen and check / read / write / ...	Höre zu und überprüfe / lies / schreibe / ...
Listen to the words / sentences / people / ...	Höre dir die Wörter / Sätze / Leute / ... an.
Look at the picture / answers / ...	Schau dir das Bild / die Antworten / ... an.
Match the pictures / ... with the sentences / ...	Ordne die Bilder / ... den Sätzen / ... zu.
Not in the text (N)?	Nicht im Text enthalten?
Practise with a partner.	Übt zu zweit.
Put a cross (✕) in the box for the wrong sentences.	Setze ein Kreuzchen ins Kästchen für die falschen Sätze.
Put a tick (✓) in the box for the correct sentences / in the correct boxes.	Setze ein Häkchen ins Kästchen für die richtigen Sätze / in die richtigen Kästchen.
Put the words in the correct order.	Bringe die Wörter in die richtige Reihenfolge.
Read about ...	Lies über ...
Read the messages / sentences / text / ...	Lies die Nachrichten / Sätze / den Text / ...
Right (✓) or wrong (✕)? / True (T) or false (F)?	Richtig oder falsch?
Swap roles.	Wechselt die Rollen.
Take turns.	Wechselt euch ab.
Talk to a partner.	Sprich mit einem/r Partner/in.
Tick (✓) the correct definition / the hobbies / ...	Hake alle richtigen Definitionen / Hobbys / ... ab.
Underline ...	Unterstreiche ...
Use the words / sentences / ... to help you.	Benutze die Wörter / Sätze / ... als Hilfe.
Use words from the box.	Benutze die Wörter aus dem Kasten.
Watch part 1 / 2 / ... (again).	Sieh dir Teil 1 / 2 / ... (nochmal) an.
Work with a partner.	Arbeitet zu zweit.
Write about six sports / your grandma / ...	Schreibe über sechs Sportarten / deine Oma / ...
Write the correct definitions / answers / sentences / ...	Schreibe die richtigen Definitionen / Antworten / Sätze / ...